Freedom's Destiny Fulfilled

Raelene Phillips

Cover Illustration by Ed French

bethel publishing

1819 S. Main, Elkhart, IN 46516

Dedication

This, my second book, is lovingly dedicated to
Danny Phillips
My boy-friend who became my man-friend
My husband, whom I lowanech!

SYNOPSIS—FREEDOM IN WHITE MITTENS

The place was Germany. The year was 1752. Sir William Stivers fell hopelessly in love with poor Hannah Duffy. Knowing that the vast difference in their stations in life made marriage impossible in their homeland, the young couple fled to America. As they were leaving Germany, a kind old lady gave Hannah some yarn which she knitted into mittens for Will. They sold themselves as indentured servants to pay for their voyage to America, agreeing to work four years upon their arrival in the New World.

The sea crossing was long and perilous, but some friendships were made which were to last a lifetime. Upon arrival in Norfolk, Virginia, the lovers were separated and sold, almost like slaves.

Will was taken to a cotton plantation where he was abused because of his strong stand for the Lord. The abuse and several bouts with malaria broke his health.

Hannah's services were bought by the Woodcutter family, whom they had met on the ship. She was treated more like a sister than a servant.

At the end of four long years, Will had changed so much that Hannah only recognized him through the mittens she had knitted for him. To Will, the mittens had become a symbol of freedom and of Hannah's undying love.

Several months after their marriage when she unravelled the mittens to make a sweater for the upcoming baby, Will's joy was complete. Now it is fourteen years later.

Chapter 1

uffy! Duffy Stivers! Come here, Duffy! I need you," Hannah shouted from the back door as she scanned the fields looking for her son. The corn had all been harvested in the nearest field. Hannah's eyes searched the fence row on the horizon as she shouted again. "Duffy! Freedom Duffy Stivers, if you can hear me, you'd better come running!"

Her face was flushed as she turned back into the kitchen mumbling to herself. "Where can that boy be? It seems that every time I need him he's off somewheres. How can I get the laundry started. . . ."

Hannah was unaware that eleven-year-old Libby had been standing in the doorway between the kitchen and the parlor. "Is Duffy gonna be in trouble, Mama?" the little girl asked.

"Libby, you startled me. I didn't know you were standing there," Hannah smiled at her daughter. With the long dark curls hanging to her waist and her sparkling blue eyes, she made quite a picture.

"Is he, Mama? Is Duffy in trouble?" The blue eyes pleaded for a negative answer, for the child nearly worshipped her older brother.

6

"Well, no," Hannah responded, patting Libby on the shoulder. "I suppose I've really no reason to be angry with your brother, for I didn't tell him to stay home today. I only just decided this morn to wash up all the clothing and I need him to draw the water for me."

Libby's face relaxed. "The only time you ever call us children by all three of our names is when you are upset with us for something, Mama. But I'm glad old Duffy's not in trouble. Sometimes I forget that his first name is Freedom." Changing the subject abruptly as she often did, Libby continued. "Let me draw the water for you, Mama. I'm big enough to do it."

"Mayhap we can work together to draw it up, Miss Liberty," Hannah replied, smiling at her daughter as she spoke.

Libby giggled as Hannah used the family's pet name for her. She took her mother's hand as they walked toward the well.

Hannah stopped suddenly and clutched at her enlarged abdomen. There were beads of perspiration on her upper lip, and she was panting.

Libby was jabbering away and didn't even seem to notice her Mama's discomfort. "And if the baby is a girl, I will make her a bonnet with lace on the edge . . . and I'll . . . Mama? Mama, what is it? Are you sick? Mama?"

"No, dear, I'm fine . . . but I've changed my mind. Mayhap I'll not do the laundry today after all. After we draw up just enough cold water for us to drink, I'll go back inside and rest whilst you go find your Papa and Duffy for me. Can you do that for your Mama?"

Libby had drawn up half a pail of water. She offered her mother the first dipperful.

"Ah, 'tis the best refreshment a body can have," Hannah murmured, beginning to pant again. Libby drank from the dipper, then turned questioning eyes to her mother.

"Libby, I think Papa and Duffy must be down in the

back forty clearing some more of those stumps. Run down and tell them to come home even though 'tis early in the day. Tell Papa I need him," Hannah said.

"Mama, you *are* sick. What is it?" a wide-eyed Libby asked.

"No, Miss Liberty," Hannah smiled, "I'm fine. But I do need your Papa. Go quickly, child."

Libby began to run toward the farthest corner of their land, turning around at the top of a rise to check on her mother.

Hannah was lumbering her bulky self into the house, stopping twice in the short distance as the birth pangs gripped her. Just as Libby turned to check on her, a pain had subsided. She waved the corner of her apron at Libby, praying the child would not worry.

"Run, child," she whispered. "Please run!"

By the time Will and Duffy came into the house, Hannah had made herself as comfortable as she could on a daybed in the kitchen.

"My lady," Will said as he fell on his knees at her side.

Hannah turned her eyes toward her husband. "It's time, my dear. Take the children over to the Wood-cutters, and uh . . . oh . . ." She gripped his hand violently.

"But Hannah, I dare not leave you. The children can just go upstairs. I want . . ."

It was one of those rare times when Hannah raised her voice. "Will, please! I will be fine. Take Duffy and Libby over to . . ."

At this point, her son interrupted her. "Mama, I'm sorry I wasn't here to draw the water," he choked. "Mama, are you going to be all right?" The tears that the thirteen-year-old boy had learned to despise so were just beneath the surface.

Hannah turned loving eyes on her firstborn. "Shh, Duffy—don't take on so. You and Libby, run and put some clothing and clean underthings in the valise. You're going to go stay with Aunt 'Cille and Uncle Marc for a few days. I'm all right.

"Is ... is ... is the baby coming?" Duffy whispered fearfully.

Hannah knew her son's mind was where hers was—in the fence-enclosed plot of ground adorned with three identical crosses, one for each of the children born to the Stivers since Libby's birth eleven years ago. Duffy could remember all three of the deaths vividly. Little James had been toddling near the edge of the yard when bitten by a poisonous snake. Duffy remembered his delirious screams long after they stopped. The other two crosses were those of babies, Elizabeth and Leah. Born just a year apart, they had lived only a few hours each. But Duffy remembered the heartbreak that came with babies.

"Duffy," Hannah murmured, gripped by another pain. "Have faith, son. It'll be different this time. Now go ... help Libby ... I'm fine." A weak smile crossed her face as Will herded the children upstairs.

In a few minutes, they were back. "My lady, I'll do as you've bidden me and bring Mistress Woodcutter back to help you. I'll hurry. Be still till I return Hannah."

"Go on," she told him with a grin. "You know this is the sixth time I've been through this. It'll be over before you know it."

Chapter 2

w, Duffy, relax, will you? You're no fun at all," complained Little Marc. "Libby isn't all worked up inside herself over the birth of this babe like you are. Babies are born every day. It's nothing to take on so about."

Libby felt she would burst with pride at these words of praise from Little Marc. Though she never admitted it, even to herself, his opinion of her was just about the most important thing in her world. She had determined years ago, at age six, that someday she would marry Little Marc Woodcutter. But of course, she had never disclosed her secret love to anyone.

"Little Marc" became more and more of a misnomer as the years passed. Of course he had been dubbed "Little" as a baby to distinguish him from his father, Mister Marcus Woodcutter, the president of Norfolk Lumber Company. But now that he was a gangly youth of fifteen, the "little" was very inappropriate. He was nearly as tall as his father, and working in the timber business had made him broad through the shoulders and very muscular. But no one ever considered his size when calling his name. He had been "Little Marc" so long that he would remain so forever.

Now Libby joined in admonishing Duffy. "Aunt 'Cille said for us children to run along down to the creek and enjoy ourselves. You're not obeying, Duffy, 'cause you're not enjoying yourself."

"Oh Libby, cut it out, will ya?" Duffy lashed out at his sister because he didn't want to offend his best friend, Little Marc. "You were so little you can't even remember when the baby girls died." Duffy was choking on under-the-surface tears. "It was the saddest thing you ever saw. I thought Mama was never gonna get over it. And besides, it's hard on Mama's health to have a baby. How can I enjoy myself when right now ..." Duffy turned his back, and his shoulders shook with sobs.

Little Marc wrapped his arm around Duffy's shoulders. "C'mon, Duffy. I know you're scared and all, but havin' babies is just natural. Why, look at my sisters. Karla and Louisa each have four. I've been an uncle so many times I can hardly keep count. And they're both healthy as horses."

Duffy brightened a little when he remembered all the brood belonging to the Witherspoon families. Just then the children heard a familiar whistle. All through the years of their childhood when they were at the Woodcutter's home, they knew Uncle Marc's whistle meant to come running.

"Race?" Little Marc asked.

"All right. I can still beat you," Duffy said as he started toward the house.

"Wait! Give me a head start—please?" Libby pleaded.

Little Marc took hold of Duffy's arm. "She *is* a girl, and a scrawny one at that," he grinned. "Take a lead to that nearest fence post, Miss Liberty. And ole' Duffy and me will still beat you to the house by a long way."

Libby ran to the fence post, then turned and shouted,

"Go!" As predicted, the boys overtook Libby in no time at all. For a while they ran abreast, but when the house came into view Duffy and Little Marc left her tasting their dust. Little Marc was larger but Duffy was much swifter. He collapsed on the back steps at Uncle Marc's feet, huffing and puffing.

"Well, Freedom," Uncle Marc began, he being the only person who never referred to Duffy by his middle name. "You've got yourself a fine brother. Your Papa said your Mama has insisted on naming the new baby after him, so his name is to be William Justice Stivers. But as we left the house your Mama was already calling the baby Willy."

As they spoke, Little Marc had arrived at the porch. The two boys embraced and jumped in a circle, patting each other on the back all the while. "It's a boy! It's a boy!" they shouted.

As Libby entered the yard, Duffy sobered and turned toward the door. "Uncle Marc, is my mama . . . is she feeling . . .?" he stammered.

"She's fine, Freedom. 'Twas the fastest and most painless delivery of a child I've e'er seen in my life. Your Aunt 'Cille wasn't even needed to help, so she came on back with me and is right now in the kitchen directing Samantha to make all your favorite foods."

Libby puffed up to the porch and Duffy grabbed her in a bear hug. "It's over! We got us a baby brother. And our Mama is fine. Isn't it grand?" he exclaimed as he swung her in a circle.

Duffy's moods often swung from the depths of despair to the highest jubilation in such a short timespan as to leave his sister dizzy. Now she panted, "Duff—put me down!" Straightening her homespun skirt and trying to regain all the composure she could in front of Little Marc, she tossed her curly head. Smiling, she remarked, "Yes, it is fine. I wonder what his name will be?"

12

Aunt 'Cille called from inside. "Libby, come on in here and I'll tell you all about him whilst we cut some quilt squares of these old dresses."

Most of the time, Libby would have preferred to stay outside with the boys. Even now, she looked longingly after Duffy and Little Marc as they headed back to the woods with fishing poles. But Aunt 'Cille was calling her again and hearing about the birth of the baby *was* enticing. And so, for once, Libby didn't mind the fact that little ladies should content themselves with learning homemaking even though fishing was ever so much more fun. "I'm coming, Aunt 'Cille!" she shouted.

* * * * * * * * * * *

The children had expected to stay with the Woodcutters for at least a week. When Mother said "a few days" it usually stretched into six or seven. The two families had grown so close during the last decade that they almost seemed like real relations. Duffy and Libby were as much at home at the Woodcutter mansion as they were at their own humbler abode. Thus it surprised everyone when Will pulled up to the front porch in the buckboard next morning.

"Duffy, Libby! Gather your things together. I've come to take ye home!"

"Will, do ya really think that's wise?" Marc asked. "Hannah may need a little time to gain her strength back. And the children are no bother."

His wife, Lucille, added, "It's a joy to have them. Let them stay another day at least."

"Well," Will said, "I don't know as but *I* agree with you. But you know Hannah! She says she feels fine and she wants her brood at home with their new brother. As fer gainin' her strength back, it don't appear that she's lost none of it. When I arose afore daybreak she had pork sidemeat and eggs a'fryin'. That wee Willy

13

had already nursed and was asleep. Hannah's just like always. She's a rarin' to go on with life. Nothin' keeps her down long."

As Will spoke his eyes seemed lit from within in the same way they had whenever he had spoken of Hannah for the last eighteen years.

"I can see there's to be no dissuading you, Will," Marc replied. "I suppose knowing Hannah's spunk mayhap ye'll have the whole family at church come Sunday?"

Will laughed as he lifted Libby onto the wagon then tossed the valise on. "If'n the babe is as healthy as he appears, I don't see no reason why we shouldn't be. I imagine Hannah is countin' on it, 'cause she was a'washing the mitten-sweater when I left home." After farewells, the Stivers headed for home.

Even though Duffy knew the story so well he could nearly repeat it with his father, he never tired of it. "Tell us again Papa. Tell us about the mitten-sweater!"

Will smiled. "I was a wealthy landowner, the son of a Lord, in Germany. Your mama was an orphan girl who worked for my family. I loved her. But they never would have allowed us to marry. So we ran away. We walked across Europe with the help of some real fine folks we met on the way."

Libby interrupted, "Like the lady who gave Mama the yarn?"

Will smiled. "Yes, Frau Hohenburger told Mama to knit herself something. But she didn't. She made me beautiful mittens instead."

Now Duffy took over the story. "And you kept those mittens during all the long four years when you and Mama were separated because you sold yourselves as indentured servants to pay your fare to America. They were like a symbol to you of Mama and love and freedom—like my first name!"

Not to be outdone by her brother, Libby said, "And

I remember that you had changed so much that Mama didn't even recognize you until you put on the mittens she had knitted when you met up again!"

Duffy retorted, "You don't either remember it. It happened before you were born. There's no way you can remember something that happened before you were born, is there Papa?"

But Will was staring far off to the west as he drove, not even hearing the bickering children. He picked up the story where Libby had left off.

"Mama unravelled my mittens and made the little sweater each of you children were christened in. She wanted all of you to be a part of our dream of freedom, so you each got to wear a garment made of that yarn from the dear little Frau who helped us get to America."

"And will our new brother Willy get christened in the special mitten-sweater, Papa?" Libby asked.

"If the good Lord is willin', we'll likely have him christened in it this comin' Sunday. As Will spoke he had pulled up at their house.

"Mama," Duffy shouted. "We're home!"

The children jumped down and ran into the house as Will unhitched the team. Hannah rose from her rocker and held the baby out to them. "Meet your new brother, William Justice," she beamed.

Chapter 3

annah's recovery from the birth of Willy was almost miraculous. But then Hannah had never been one to baby herself. Will was not allowing her to do any heavy lifting, and Duffy and Libby were very solicitous of their Mama. It helped also that Willy was an extremely docile baby. He nursed slowly, was cleaned and changed, and slept peacefully—either in the cradle or one of the little family's willing arms. Hannah feared the baby would be spoiled beyond words, but Will thought he was too young to be spoiled.

There was much discussion about the upcoming christening. "What if it is too cold to take the baby out, Will? He does appear to be a mite weaker than the other children were," Hannah worried.

"Oh, my lady, will you never learn not to worry?" Will gently chided. "If 'tis too cold, we'll simply wait 'til the first nice Sunday. The vicar will understand. It probably makes him no difference when we christen the lad. Matter of fact, I saw him out front of the feed and grain store in town yesterday and he said he would be surprised if we *are* there this comin' Sunday.

You know most women don't get up and around after the birth of a babe as quick-like as you do."

Libby had entered the sitting room during their conversation. "Why do we have to have him christened anyway? We all know what his name is already."

Hannah chuckled. "Libby, the christening is sort of a formal ceremony thanking God for giving us baby Willy."

"But why does the vicar have to put that yucky stuff on him? I don't understand," the little girl pouted.

"Oh, Libby, that part is just a sign or a symbol to the world. It's just a little drop or two of oil that he puts on the baby's forehead," Hannah responded.

Will interrupted because he had always taken very seriously his responsibility to be the spiritual leader in his home. "Come here, Lib. Sit on Papa's lap."

When the little girl was all settled he continued. "In the Bible, oil is oft a picture or a symbol of God's Holy Spirit. And so you see, when the vicar puts a drop of oil on a baby's forehead, it is like a picture of hoping that the child will always let the Spirit of God have control of him. Do you understand?"

"I think. I hope God's Spirit is in control in me. Is it?" The innocence in those big blue eyes as she looked at her Papa nearly confounded Will.

"Whenever you want God's Spirit to be in control, Lib, then it is. I hope you always will want that." He playfully pulled one of the curls hanging over her shoulders. "And now, enough about the up and comin' christening . . . answer me a question. What are two of the most important things in the new world?"

Libby grinned. It was a game Papa had begun when she was just a toddler barely able to talk, one he had played with Duffy before her. "Oh, Papa!" she squirmed, thinking young ladies of eleven were too big for such silliness.

"I'll not let you go till ya give me my answer," he

said as he squeezed her tightly. "C'mon now, what are the two important things?"

Libby rolled her eyes but the dimples showed that she was enjoying the old game. "All right," she giggled. "The two most important things are freedom and liberty."

"And who are two very important people?" Papa asked.

"Freedom Duffy Stivers and Liberty Lucille Stivers!" She giggled as he tickled her.

"It 'pears to me ya ought to add our new brother to the old game," said a low voice in the doorway.

"Oh, good mornin' Duffy," Hannah said. "Is the chorin' all done?"

"Yes'm," he replied. He turned to his papa. "Mayhap ya ought to ask what are three important things here in America now."

"Yer right son. What would the answer be then, Libby?"

For a moment the girl looked confused. "Oh, I get it," she responded then. "The three important things would be Freedom, Liberty, and Justice. And besides me and Duffy, the third important person would be William Justice Stivers. Right?"

* * * * * * * * * * *

There had been frost on the ground for two nights, but Sunday morning the sun had a summertime warmth to it.

"Oh, isn't it a beautiful day?" Hannah asked as they neared the church.

"Couldn't have asked for a more gorgeous one, eh, my lady?" Hannah knew Will was reminding her again of how she had fretted earlier. And truly, there wasn't a cloud in view. The sky was so blue it nearly hurt your eyes to look at it. The frost had encouraged colors in the

18

trees. The woods they drove through just before reaching the edge of Norfolk had shades of brown, gold, orange, and red with just enough green left for contrast. The bittersweet on the fence posts was fully open now. 'Twas such a crispy clear day that in truth Hannah almost hated to go inside the new little church building on the edge of town. But the bell was ringing as Will lifted Hannah down from the wagon.

The service proceeded as usual through the Scripture reading, hymns, and prayer. Then came the moment the Stivers had been waiting for.

"We have the joy of welcoming into our church family today a new little member of the Stivers family. Will and Hannah, would you and the baby's Godparents care to step forward?"

There were a few moments of confusion as Will ushered his wife and baby out of their pew. Hannah wore what Will said was her best-looking dress, one she had fashioned of royal blue velvet. It boasted a five inch wide collar of lace she had tatted herself. There were also lace insets in the full sleeves which were gathered into wide cuffs. Hannah had also taken extra time this morning plaiting her hair into two long braids and then twisting them into a coronet effect around her head. There were just enough white hairs among the dark brown to give Hannah a look of maturity without making her look old.

Will also had dressed with special care this morning. His suit was dark brown wool. The jacket was double-breasted with four gold-colored buttons. His stock was ecru and boasted an edging of brown lace down each ruffle. The shirt was his only "store-bought" one, a Christmas gift from their special friend, Captain Phillip Woodcutter, the previous year. Hannah had added the edging of brown lace to the ruffles to make the shirt match the suit and the brown ascot. He did look distinguished, in spite of his slight limp and the stoop to his shoulders. His prematurely white hair was pulled into a queue at the nape of his neck, according to the fashions of the day. And his clean-shaven face beamed with pride as he slowly ushered Hannah to the front of the church, followed by the Woodcutters.

The center of everyone's attention was the baby in Hannah's arms. Though only five days old the tiny face was that of a wise old man. He stared at his world from large eyes the color of indigo. And when he puckered his face in a certain way there was the hint of a dimple in his left cheek. He wore a simple gown of white flannel free of any adornment save a row of embroidered light blue hearts and flowers around the hem. And on top the gown was the oft-spoken-of sweater knitted of yarn which had originally been his father's mittens. He had a square jaw line, a perfect rosebud mouth, a little button nose, and lots of coal black hair peeked from under the edge of the little bonnet made by his sister.

The congregation tried to listen as the vicar explained this ceremony as an act of dedicating this child to the Lord as the Biblical Hannah had done with her son, Samuel. But in truth everyone was craning their necks for a clearer view of the baby. Now the vicar took the wee child into his arms and prayed a quick prayer of thanksgiving and blessing. Then he dipped his finger in a little vial of oil and touched it against the baby's forehead. Willy began to fuss weakly, his little fist trashing in the air. There was an audible sigh from the entire congregation at his cry. Even the stately vicar was smiling as he said, "And what is the child to be called?"

Hannah and Will spoke together, "His name is William Justice Stivers."

"And who are the Godparents of this child?"

"Mistress Woodcutter and myself," said Marc as he stepped forward a bit.

"And do you, Marcus and Lucille, promise to see to

it that this babe is brought up in the fear and admonition of the Lord?"

"We do," they responded quietly.

The parson then prayed again for the future of the baby, ending the ceremony in the ancient form. "And so, I christen thee, William Justice Stivers, in the name of the Father, the Son, and the Holy Ghost."

Hannah was more tired from the trip to church than she was willing to admit. But she finally did concede to Will's suggestion that she go to bed early that evening. She reflected on the memories of these days since Willy's birth as she fell asleep. A smile crossed her face as she thought of Libby, the little mother-hen who saw no reason the baby should ever be allowed to cry. Duffy seemed so grown-up, all of a sudden shouldering more and more responsibility of the farm. He was more relaxed than she had seen him in months and she realized regretfully how deeply he had worried about her and the baby. When her mind turned to her husband and the new baby, her brow was furrowed. There was something bothering her, but she couldn't give a name to any specific problem. Will seemed a bit restless these days; often he stood staring westward. As to baby Willy, he nursed too weakly she was sure.

"Lord, I'm too tired for real prayin'," she whispered. "Just take care of everything." Before she even thought the "Amen", she was asleep.

Chapter 4

illy was now nearly a month old and everyone was beginning to admit that there was indeed some kind of problem with the baby. He needed to nurse every couple hours around the clock, and half of what he took in came back out as he spit up constantly.

"Mayhap my milk just doesn't agree with him," Hannah confided her fears to Lucille, Karla, and Louisa one day when they came to visit.

"I don't know," commented Karla. "I've never had me any problems like this with my children." Hannah looked almost envious as she stared through the window to where Karla's three chubby blond younger children ran and raced with Louisa's three and Libby in the yard. Duffy and Little Marc were off by themselves somewhere. Louisa's eldest daughter, fourteen-year-old Hannah, and Karla's eldest, Marta, sat demurely with the adults working on cross-stitch samplers.

Louisa asked, "Hannah, have you had Doctor Hatfield look at the baby?"

The doctor was the one who had tended to Will's leg years ago when he was detained by a bad break on his trip to join Hannah in Norfolk. He had recently moved to Norfolk to be near his daughter, Eleanor, who had married a fisherman. The Stivers and Woodcutters and Witherspoons had been his first patients in the area, helping him to build a large family practice via their words of praise for him.

Hannah replied despairingly, "Yes, Will had the doctor to come out earlier this week. He confirmed my fears. The baby just isn't gaining any weight and isn't very strong. We are trying to keep it from the children, but I think Duffy is beginnin' to suspect that somethin' bad is wrong." Her voice began to break. "Doc Hatfield said that short of a miracle we aren't goin' to be able to raise little Willy."

Her little namesake laid down her stitchery and came over to hug her. "Don't despair, Aunt Hannah. Mama told me that you always taught her and Aunt Karla that God answers prayer. Whyn't we pray right now for Willy?"

At the suggestion of the teenager, the ladies all bowed their heads for a season of prayer. Each in turn besought the Lord on behalf of the baby who just was not thriving.

As the ladies were beginning to leave, young Hannah made another suggestion. "What about cow's milk?"

"We already tried, dear. It didn't work. I tried mixing it with some of my own milk. I tried whole milk. I tried it without the cream. I tried adding water ... nothing seems to work. Willy spits up no matter what we try."

Once again that night Hannah and Will were discouraged as they prepared for bed. On their knees togther they poured out their longings to God. Will ended the prayer, "Oh, God, if there's a way to find help for our Willy, please show us that way. But Lord we also want to be willin' ... so nevertheless, not our will, but thine be done. Amen."

Hannah had been nestled against Will as she slept so her quick movement startled him awake.

"Goats!" she exclaimed.

"Hannah, what on earth?" Will mumbled. " 'Tis the middle of the night. Ya must be dreamin'. Lie back down, my lady."

"But Will, I think I've got the answer. Mayhap it even came from the Lord. It's goats!"

"Hannah, have you gone daft? What are you talking about?"

Hannah was so excited she had gone to the fireplace and using a long taper had lit an oil lamp. Will stared at her incredulously. She was flitting around the room excitedly.

"Can't you see, Will? The answer is goats."

Still sleepy, he asked, "The answer to what?"

"For Willy. Darling, I did have a dream. In the dream we were back in Germany. We were just leavin' Frau Hohenburger's house, riding in the cart on our trip to freedom. You surely remember, Will."

"Well, of course, I remember," her husband replied, still eyeing Hannah worriedly. "But what has that to do with the baby?"

"Think back very carefully, dear. It will come to you just as it did to me, I'm sure!" Hannah said excitedly. "Remember riding on the cart?"

"Yes, the cart was full of cans and jars of goat's milk which the boy collected twice each week."

"Do you remember why he came?"

Will looked thoughtful. "He came to get the milk for his family who lived just across the border in Holland. He came . . . oh, yes, my lady, now I understand!" Will exclaimed. "Frau said the lad had a baby brother who could not tolerate any kind of milk but goat's milk. Oh, Hannah, do you really think . . ." He left the hope unstated.

"Well, Will, all I know is we've asked and asked for

divine help for Willy. Then tonight I had that dream. I've never before dreamed so vividly nor been able to remember it so clearly. We were getting into the cart to leave the Frau's house. She had packed us such a wondrous lunch. Then she gave me the white yarn. And, as we climbed aboard, she explained why the lad was there each week for goat's milk. I heard and saw it all so plainly. Will, could it be that our Willy could thrive and grow on goat's milk?" Her voice had dropped to an awe-struck whisper.

The very next morning Will went to the country where he began searching the farmyards, pens, and fields for goats. At the close of the day he had secured two nannies, a billy, and a half-grown kid. He very gingerly began to milk the nannies, but relaxed when he found that they gave their milk easily and generously.

The whole family gathered around as Hannah offered baby Willy the first bottle. He sucked with more vigor than he'd ever shown. Hannah stopped him twice to burp him. Duffy and Libby held their breath, for this was when the baby usually spit up all he had taken. The baby burped quickly, only losing a tiny bubble of the goat's milk. He continued to drink until he drained the bottle. Hannah's eyes were full of tears of gratitude as she placed Willy in his cradle. "Now, if only he can *keep* it down," she whispered.

The next several hours were anxious ones. Willy did not wake up. Two hours elapsed and he didn't fuss or want to nurse. Then four hours. Hannah wondered if there was any such thing as a poisonous goat. Had they *killed* Willy? But no, the child was breathing. Six hours elapsed. Not only was Hannah beside herself with worry, she was also uncomfortable until she hand-expressed her own milk. Fourteen hours elapsed before Willy finally awoke with a lusty cry. He had been checked and rechecked to make sure he was alive.

25

Again he guzzled a bottleful of the goat's milk.

The change in the baby was miraculous. Within a week a loud cry had replaced the pathetic whimpers of the first month of his life. In two weeks his weight had nearly doubled, and for the first time Hannah had hope that they were going to be able to raise Willy after all.

The addition of goats to the farm added excitement. Libby had named the goats and was treating them as her own personal pets. The billy was dubbed Herbert, the nannies were Henrietta and Harriet, and the kid was called Jonah. Duffy and Will built a pen for the goats near the barn, but it seemed Herbert could break out of any fence. The smallest noise would spook the goats and Herbie would break the fence and they would be gone. It became common for Duffy and Libby to be combing the countryside, calling for the goats. It was a game to the children and the goat family would trot home at the children's heels as tame as a dog. Libby taught Jonah to come when called and even to jump over small objects on command.

So, besides saving Willy's life, the goats brought the family much joy and entertainment. And when Hannah made a batch of goat's milk fudge, everyone agreed that the goats were the best investment they had ever made.

Chapter 5

hanksgiving of 1770 had come and gone with no celebration of any kind at the Stivers' home. Those had been the darkest days, when everyone was sure Willy would be gone within hours. They had all been so fearful that no one had even mentioned the holiday. Truthfully, Hannah had indeed forgotten it.

But now that Willy was so much better and everyone relaxed, Hannah spoke to the family after supper one evening.

"Duffy, Libby, how would you like to accompany me into Norfolk tomorrow?"

Shocked faces turned toward hers. "My lady, what do you need in town?" Will asked. "Just write me up a list and I'll get anything you be a needin'."

"So sorry, dear husband," Hannah retorted. "You cannot do this shopping. If my memory and the calendar are correct, 'tis only ten days until we shall celebrate Christmas. Hence, I must do the shopping."

The children were grinning from ear to ear. "Oh, yes, Mama, I want to go." Libby bounced with excitement as she spoke. "I have saved fourteen cents and I too

27

need to do some very special shopping." Her eyes sparkled with the joy of Christmas secrets.

Now Will raised a new objection. "But what about baby Willy? Who will care for. . . ."

The mischievous grin on Hannah's face gave him his answer before he finished the question.

"Oh, Hannah, dear, . . . I don't know. What if he spits up again? Or what if I get the bottle too warm? I'm not even sure I know how to change his little britches. He's awful tiny yet."

Hannah laughed aloud. "Aye, my love, he is awful tiny and it's ashamed you should be that such a little baby can turn you into a mountain of mush. I'll have his bottle all ready afore we go. Oh, Will, don't take on so," she giggled at her husband's restlessness. "We'll only be gone an hour or so. It's not like the olden days when Norfolk was nigh half a day's drive away. Why the town is almost at our doorstep. I'm sure you can handle Willy the short length of time our shopping will take us. Duffy, can you handle the team?"

"Yes, Mama. And I have the twenty-five cent piece that Captain Phil gave me last year for Christmas. So I will do some shopping too."

After the breakfast chores were all done, Hannah and the two older children bundled into the buckboard and headed for town. Will stood in the doorway giving instructions to Duffy until a cry came from the cradle.

"His bottle is on the hearth," Hannah shouted as Duffy cracked the mare on the back and the wagon jolted away from the porch. "Good luck, Papa," she grinned.

Several new shopping districts had emerged as the town of Norfolk outgrew its boundaries time after time. Hannah instructed Duffy to drive on past the first three shops where she could have made her purchases, explaining that one must be frugal and pursue the best prices. Soon Duffy pulled up in front of a freshly white-washed building bearing the sign, "McMaster's General Store." Each of the shoppers had pre-determined gift selections which interested them. Once inside the store, they scattered into aisles far apart.

Duffy was leaning over a counter of cutlery, examining a whetstone. When he and his father cut brush and weeds in the far back forty of their land, his papa's tools often became dull. Duffy couldn't count the times papa had said, "Would that I had a small whetstone to carry with me, so's I could resharpen this ax (or knife or saw) without waiting until we get back to the barn."

Mr. McMaster came to wait on him.

"What's the price of that smallest whetstone?" the boy asked.

"Ah, 'tis a fine handy tool to have," answered the Scot. "See 'ere—this side is whetstone. T'other side be pure flint. So's a body can sharpen tools or start a fire when out workin' in the woods."

"It's fine, I agree," Duffy retorted. "My papa sure would like it. The price?"

Sizing up the lad and noting the eagerness in his eyes, the soft-hearted Scotsman asked, "What'd ye be willin' to pay, lad?" He had nonchalantly bumped over the price posted near the rock which clearly read 50¢.

"I've only twenty-five cents to spend and I wanted to get Mama and my sister something. And then there's the baby. . . ." His voice trailed off as a very dejected Libby sidled up to him.

"What's wrong, Lib?" He interrupted his own conversation.

"Oh, I wanted to get Mama some pretty lace to trim a bonnet with, but it costs ten cents and that'd only leave me four cents to spend on Papa." Her blue eyes stood full of tears, ready to spill over at any moment.

Mr. McMaster had listened to this exchange and stood marvelling at the children's unselfish attitudes. "I've a dandy idea, younguns. I'm presumin' me that the two of ya are brother and sister." As Duffy and Libby nodded, he continued. "Whyn't ya pool yer funds, so to speak, and that way ya can get both the items for yer folks."

Libby brightened. "Why, sure—I have fourteen and Duffy has twenty-five cents so that makes . . . ummm . . . uh . . ."

Duffy spoke up. "Thirty-nine cents! I like the idea, sir, but I still don't know. How much for the whet-flint stone?"

Mr. McMaster thought for a minute. "Let's say twenty cents. And with the lace that comes to thirty cents. Ya've nine cents left."

The children stepped back a couple steps and whispered to each other, with Libby pointing all the while to another row of shelves covered with toys. McMaster sighed. He thought he'd come across two truly unselfish young people, but now realized they also wanted something for themselves. He was about to rescind his generous offer when Duffy spoke.

"Pardon me, sir . . . but my sister says there's a toy over there that our baby could shake and make noise. What is its price, please?"

"I'll let ya have it for nine cents, since ye're such good customers," the storekeeper smiled.

Libby nearly jumped for joy. "Won't Christmas be grand, Duffy?" she exclaimed as she pulled her fourteen cents out of the tiny reticule. The three purchases were wrapped in brown paper and tied with string, and the children turned to the front of the store.

Unbeknown to them, as they were dickering prices with the happy Scotsman, Hannah had purchased several pieces of yardgoods. A dress length for Libby of pale pink calico, some lovely white linen for handkerchiefs for Duffy, and some beautifully tanned leather for a jacket for Will. She would have hours of work ahead of her. But with Willy sleeping better and the children in school most of each day, she felt certain she could finish her projects in time for the holiday. Will was fashioning a wooden toy duck for Willy, so it should prove a happy Christmas indeed. Gathering up her purchases, Hannah started for the door.

"C'mon Duffy—Libby—time to go," she said as she turned into the last aisle.

"Oh, my," said a pretty lady as she stepped backward to avoid a collision with Hannah.

"I'm sorry," Hannah blushed.

"No, 'tis my fault," came the retort in a thick German accent. "Aach! Can it be? Me thinks—oh Hannah—it is! Aren't you Hannah?"

"Yes, 'tis my given name, but . . . I fear I don't know you," the flustered Mrs. Stivers responded.

"Look at me close, Hannah. We all thought you were dead. You just disappeared." Seeing that her cousin still did not recognize her, she spoke again. "Hannah, it's me—yer cousin, Katrina!"

'Twas a good thing there was a cracker barrel with lid closed directly behind Hannah. She blanched white as the snow which had begun to fall lightly, and staggering backwards plopped ungracefully atop the barrel.

"Can it be?" she mumbled. But even as her mouth uttered the question, her brain registered the truth. Surely this lovely young lady in the fur cape standing before her was her cousin from Germany.

"Mama, what is it? Are you all right?" the children's voices registered the concern they felt when, upon rounding the corner of the last aisle-way, they saw their mama sitting atop a cracker barrel, struggling valiantly to regain her normal composure.

"Hannah!" squealed Katrina. "Are these darling children your'n? But of course they are. This girl is the very image of you, ceptin' for the black hair." As she spoke she took hold of Hannah's hands which had dropped all her packages. "Oh, Hannah, please be glad to see me. I know we treated you horrible all those years ago. But can you forgive that? You . . . you're the only blood relation I've got left alive in the world . . . and I didn't even know you was alive." Here Katrina's eyes filled with tears, and something stirred inside Hannah. She could tell that speaking in English was new and foreign to the girl, nay—lady, standing before her. After a quick word to the children to take the packages to the buckboard, she spoke softly in German.

"Aach, Katrina, 'tis me that needs your forgiveness for running away as I did all those years ago. But what happened to Uncle Peter and all the others?"

The two ladies moved outside as they spoke, catching up on nearly eighteen years in just a few moments. Hannah learned to her chagrin that after Katrina married, a strange sort of ague had moved through the serfs' cottages back at Stivers' Castle in Germany, leaving a trail of death behind. Katrina's voice broke as she explained. "They all died the same day, Hannah. Mama and Papa, Gertrude, and Peter Junior. Oh, I know they were cruel taskmasters to you, Hannah, but it still hurts me so to think of it after all these years."

Libby and Duffy waited wide-eyed in the buckboard which Hannah now leaned upon, with her arm across the strange German lady's shoulders. Suddenly Hannah realized that it was snowing quite hard and made a difficult decision.

"Katrina, I'm sorry but I have a tiny baby at home left in my husband's care. So I must be going. Could you possibly come with us to my house so's we could get all caught up?" she asked, looking around for a wagon and wondering how Katrina came to be in that store.

"Oh, could I? My husband is having our horses reshod at the livery over yonder. We are moving farther west and I came in here to buy supplies. Mayhap he could come and meet you and your'n later?"

After a brief conference with Katrina's husband, giving directions to the Stivers' house and insisting that he come join them for supper, the buckboard was headed home. Hannah made very brief introductions of her cousin to the children. Then the two ladies conversed in fast fluent German all the way home.

Chapter 6

ate that evening with the children long alseep, Will and Hannah sat before the fire.

"I know that I've said it o'er and o'er, yet I must repeat it again. 'Tis still nigh impossible for me to believe," Hannah said with a shake of her head.

"Yes, it nearly confounds a person for sure," Will agreed. "To think that after all these years and all the distance we came, you'd e'er come face to face with your kin again! If they hadn't stopped in Norfolk on their westward journey . . . and if they'd a-stopped at any of t'other stores or blacksmiths . . . why, my lady, I'd say yer meeting Katrina today was nigh a miracle.

"When I think that they were just passin' through, it does seem providential," Hannah smiled. She seemed happy, considering the loss of her entire family. "Adolph seems a likeable chap. He certainly is excited about goin' west."

Will suddenly became animated. "I understand that, my lady. Norfolk is gettin' too big fer its britches . . . too sophisticated to suit me. And the town . . . why, she's practically poundin' on our front door." Will walked around the room and swung his arm toward the western wall. "The future of this country of America lies in the west, Hannah. I ... why, I'd give my right arm to be a goin' west with Adolph and Katrina in the mornin'."

For the first time Hannah was able to put a name to the strange emotion that gripped her heart when Will seemed distant and stared at the far horizon so regularly. It was fear.

She dropped her eyes so he couldn't see the tears under the surface. Her voice was barely more than a mumble. "But Will, I thought you *liked* our farm and our home. I ne'er dreamed you longed to go farther west."

Will tried to shrug off the fervor with which he'd spoken of the West. "Oh, my lady, don't worry. I'm content enough here ... 'tis just that ... but never mind. Mayhap I was just born with ramblin' blood."

"Speaking of your blood," Hannah interrupted, glad for a change of subject, "what will you do about your mother?"

Will sat staring into the fire again as he spoke.

"I've been thinkin' on that e'er since yer cousin left. Who e'er would've dreamed back when we left Germany that my brother would die? I doubt I would've had the gumption to leave if I'd known Mother would be left alone."

Hannah suddenly looked awestruck. "Why, Will ... it just came to me ... mayhap you're a very rich man ... or you will be someday. Wouldn't yer brother's death make you the heir apparent to Stivers' Castle?"

Will nodded. "Yes, I'd already thought on that. But remember, Katrina and Adolph said they all believe me to be dead. I wouldn't want the castle or the riches. But it does bother me to think that Mother thinks she has no one left, when she really has a son, a wonderful daughter-in-law, and three beautiful grandchildren."

"Mayhap we could send word to her somehow."

"We'll think on it," Will said as he banked the fire

for the night. "Come, my lady. I know it's been a grand day for reunionizing for you. But Willy will still have to be fed at dawn."

Will was asleep as soon as his head hit the pillow. But Hannah thought long into the night. Was Will really happy, or would he want to follow the ranks of so many others and join America's westward expansion? Hannah loved her home, her friends, her neighbors. Could she sacrifice all this for Will's peace of mind? And what of Indians? Finally she fell into a troubled sleep.

* * * * * * * * * * *

The next nine days passed quickly and Christmas was upon the Stivers before they knew it. As they had all through the preceding years, they joined the Woodcutters to celebrate the day. Gifts were exchanged all around. Fantastic food had been devoured. Now 'twas mid-afternoon and the day grew quiet. Babies were napping, children played games outside, and the adults were ready to doze off.

"Captain Phil, when will ya be makin' yer next voyage to the homeland?" Will asked Marc Woodcutter's brother.

"I'm plannin' to leave next week, Will. Any special reason ya be askin'?"

Hannah's heart stood still. In her own daily time of reading God's Word and praying, she had asked God repeatedly to let Will see that he should contact his mother somehow. She felt that since the news Katrina had given them, Will would never truly relax again until he let his mother know that he was alive and well. Instinctively, however, she sensed that this was a decision Will must make for himself. So, while she daily had asked God to guide him, she talked it over with no one else. Now she felt like jumping for joy as Will continued.

"Well, Cap'n, yes. There is a reason. You remember I'm sure that when Hannah and I made our voyage on the *Wedgewood* with ya all those long years ago, we were sort of runnin' away. Not that we'd committed any crime or anything—'twas just that my rich family would never have allowed me to marry my lady."

Captain Phil colored slightly. "Aye, I can see why ye would've been willin' to leave yer riches for the likes of Mistress Hannah." Both men smiled remembering that once long ago Captain Phil had also loved Hannah. Though that love was now nothing more than a memory, evidently Captain Phil Woodcutter had never given his heart to another for he remained a bachelor.

"Anyway," Will continued, "we've recently had news that my elder brother has passed on. That makes me, and Hannah and the children, the only livin' kin my mother has. I'm still not interested in the inheritance, nor the castle. I could never enjoy something I hadn't worked for with my own hands. But I've been thinkin' mayhap I ought to at least let her know I'm alive."

"Interestin' Will . . . cause I've been thinkin' that on this next voyage of mine I'd like to see me a bit more of Europe than usual. Thought as I might just port the old *Wedgewood* in Amsterdam and do me some traipsin' around the continent. So how's about if I hand-deliver the letter ye'll write to the Castle in Germany. That is, providin' ye can give me directions of how to find it."

Will grew excited. He strode over to pound the Captain on the back, thanking him repeatedly and motioning to Hannah to get their things together.

"It's beginnin' to get dark, my lady. And we've a long letter to compose when we get home. It'll take some rememberin' to get the phrasin' right in German after all these years of speakin' only English."

Goodbyes were said, and arrangements made for

Captain Phil to stop at the Stivers' home on the morrow to pick up the letter. Duffy brought the wagon around and they left for home amidst cries of "Merry Christmas."

"Papa, if the snow continues, mayhap come Sunday we can ride to church in the sleigh," Duffy hoped.

"Could be," Will responded. "Miss Liberty, yer awful quiet. Didn't you have a merry Christmas?"

"Oh, Papa, it was wonderful. I thank you and Mama ever so much for my new dress. Little Marc said he liked it—that it made me look all growed up. And isn't this bracelet that he gave me beautiful?"

Hannah turned to remark again on Little Marc's carving ability, the bracelet Libby referred to being a ring of walnut wood carved into perfect rosettes. But she was stopped short when she saw Libby's face. "Why, my little girl is nigh becomin' a woman," Hannah thought. This new realization gave Hannah much to ponder, hoping her friendship with Little Marc wouldn't hurt Libby in the future. Hannah's mind continued on this track until they pulled up in front of their home.

Amid all the hubbub of carrying in their Christmas gifts from the Woodcutters and getting a bottle of goats' milk into crying baby Willy, Will whispered to Hannah, "Is somethin' amiss, my lady? You were awful quiet ridin' home."

Hannah forced herself to brighten. "No, Will. It's been a lovely day. I was just wool-gatherin'."

Late that evening when the children were in bed, Will and Hannah sat at the table with the lamp between them, its wick turned as high as possible without smoking the glass. They talked for a long time before Will dictated this letter which Hannah painstakingly wrote out for him to send with the Captain on the morrow. In the best high German on a clean sheet of parchment it read,

Dearest Mother,

I know this letter will come as quite a shock to you as you have believed me to be dead for many years. I hope you will be happy to learn that I am not dead.

Mother, please try to understand what I am about to say. I know that you wanted only the best for me all those years ago when you set up the marriage of convenience for me with the Duchess of Blockberg. I do understand how our wedding would have doubled the fortunes of Stivers' Castle. But Mother, you never consulted me, and I hope you can understand what I am about to say. I did not love the Duchess. My heart belonged to little Hannah Duffy, who worked our land, living with her Uncle Peter in cottage number 8. Knowing you would never understand my reasoning, I took a coward's way and ran away to America. Miss Hannah came with me, Mother . . . and she is all I've ever wanted as a wife. We live on a small farm on the edge of a growing city called Norfolk here in the area of the New World known as Virginia. Mother, we have three lovely children. Duffy, our son, is thirteen years old. Libby, a daughter, is eleven. And we have a new baby, Willy. So you see, Mother, you are not alone in the world. (We recently learned of the death of Charles.) You have a wonderful family waiting here to love you.

And so, Mother, that brings me to the real point of this letter. My wife and I have talked this over at length and are in perfect agreement. We want you to sell the castle and come and live with us here in America. Please weigh carefully all the advantages of our proposition. Don't just say no. We really desperately want you to come.

The man who will give you this letter is Captain of the Ship Wedgewood, on which we made our crossing. He will help you make arrangements. We shall anxiously await his next arrival in Norfolk, hoping mayhap you will be with him. Or, at the very least, a letter from you stating your future journey plans.

Mother, there is so much I want to say to you, but feel compelled to keep this letter short and to the point. Please forgive the rash actions of a young man in love eighteen years ago. And come to us so that we may share our lives with you. The God that you taught me to love is still Lord of my life. And I pray that He will bring you safely to me.

Your loving son,
William

Chapter 7

he snow which had begun to fall late in the afternoon on Christmas continued. When Captain Phil stopped the next day to pick up Will's letter, Libby and Duffy were just putting the finishing touches on a snowman in the front yard.

"What say ye, ole Duffy?" the Captain shouted. " 'Tis a grand snow for packin', eh?" as he fired a large snowball at Duffy's head.

The children immediately left off their building and began to pummel the Captain with snowballs as he secured his horse and headed for the door.

"Children! Children! Where're yer manners?" Hannah shouted over their giggles as she bid the Captain enter. "I'm sorry, Phillip. You'd think they never saw snow afore," she mumbled, embarrassed.

"Aach-nay, 'tis me own fault. I started it," he laughed. "But I doubt they e'er have seen this much snow afore. The northern colonies refer to Virginia as 'The South'. I do believe in all my trips to America I've ne'er seen this much snow this far south afore."

"Well, the children are certainly enjoyin' it," Hannah responded as she offered both Will and their guest a

40

cup of hot tea.

"Nay, none for me," the Captain answered. "I'm in a bit of a hurry. The letter . . . and the directions?"

Hannah left the menfolk alone and went back to her mending. When the tea was ready she took a cup in to Will, and found both men standing at the door.

"Then it should be about three months at the earliest or five or six at the longest, right Phil?" Will asked.

"Aye," he answered already slipping back into his sea-faring lingo. "With favorable winds and no trouble findin' yer home, I could be back in March. But don't count on it until April or May."

"Till then, Godspeed," Will replied. He and Hannah stood at the doorway waving to their friend and laughing as the children again threw some well-aimed snowballs.

"Come Libby, Duffy! You've been out long enough. Time to get into dry duds afore ye catch yer death." Hannah herded the children into the kitchen and began to rub Libby's hair with a towel.

The snow fell softly all evening and the temperature plummeted steadily. Then near morning, a fierce wind began to howl around the eaves of the house.

At first light the next morn, Duffy opened the kitchen door. "Mama! Look!" he shouted.

Huge snowflakes were whirling in every direction at the same time. The land looked unfamiliar. What should have been shrubs were little mountains of white. One could just barely see a shadow where the barn should be.

"Bundle yourself good, Son. The wind makes it seem so much colder," Will told Duffy as he prepared to do his morning chores.

What was normally a short sprint from the house to the barn was a trying ordeal for the lad. As soon as he got away from the shelter of the house, the wind smacked him broadside almost knocking him down.

Leaning into the wind and walking at a side angle, Duffy finally got to the barn. The snow piled against the door was knee deep. In his rush to leave the house, he'd jammed his hands into the pockets of his britches. Now he longed for his mittens which hung near the kitchen stove to dry. He could think of no other way to get the door open, so he plunged his bare hands into the snow and shovelled a little area to pull the door open. He was about to despair of ever accomplishing the task when a great tree branch hit the barn door.

"Whew. That only missed me a mite," Duffy shouted. But the wind wrenched the words from his mouth, turning the shout into a whisper. "Providential," he muttered, using the tree branch as a broom to sweep and rake the snow away from the door.

Eventually he tugged the barn door open just enough for his slim young figure to enter. Running toward the hay, he shouted as he always did, "Herbert! Henrietta, Harriet! C'mon Jonah! Aren't you hungry?" Usually the goats were so glad to know they'd be set free outside in the morning, that they nearly knocked him down.

Duffy stood stock still, as the realization hit him. The goats were gone! A blast of cold air and snow from the north end of the barn caught his attention as the shutter on the only window in the barn smashed outward. Of course! The hay was piled near this window. It would have been an easy leap for any of the four goats to clear the window from the hay.

"Dumb stupid goats!" Duffy grumbled as he re-hooked the shutters on the window. But he felt immediate remorse as he remembered the hours of fun the goats had given him and Libby. "Where could they be in a blizzard like this?" he wondered aloud.

Duffy carefully milked the cow, but knew he could never carry the bucket of milk outside so he placed a clean burlap bag over the bucket and sat it in the corner of the barn. He threw down hay for the horses and cow, then rebundled himself against the ferocious storm.

The boy struggled valiantly to open the barn door again. Once outside, he paused to get his bearings. Where the house should be was a blinding wall of white. Head down, hands in pockets, he trudged into the brightness. After what seemed like hours, he stumbled over a drop-off and fell headlong. When he finally pushed the snow off his face and forced his eyes open, he realized he had misjudged the angle he should walk. Missing the house entirely, he had now stumbled over a small bricked embankment and was lying right at the door to the springhouse.

Though nearly frozen through, even Duffy could see the irony of his error. "Providential," he grinned, as he shoved open the door of the springhouse. For since the goats were missing, making it impossible for him to milk, he would need to get milk for the baby from the springhouse. "May as well do it all in one trip, rather than get all warm and then have to come back out here as soon as Willy wakes," he told himself as he struggled to find a way to carry three glass bottles of the precious milk. "Mayhap 'tis a good thing Mama always makes our clothing big enough to last a while," he grinned as he carefully placed the three bottles inside his coat, tucking the coat into his britches so the bottles couldn't fall out. Duffy didn't ordinarily talk to himself. But something about this crazy blizzard made it seem as if he was all alone in the world. He felt he must talk to himself, or else go mad.

Once again outside, Duffy squinted toward the house. "It's not that far," he muttered and leaned into the wind again. With his left arm he cradled the bottles which bounced against his body with each step. His right arm he held straight in front of him, knowing after the fall at the springhouse that the snow was so blinding he might walk into something and not even see it. As he walked he silently prayed, "God, please help me. And be with the dumb stupid goats!"

When his hand struck the house he could have cried tears of joy. It took him a minute to realize it was the side of the house. As soon as he understood where he was, he began to flail through the snow never losing touch with the house and shouting as he realized he was on the porch. "Mama! Papa! Help!"

His parents brought the cold, wet, confused boy into the warm kitchen.

"The goats . . ." he began. "They're gone! And I got lost and couldn't find the house. But 'twas a good thing because the baby needed milk and I fell at the springhouse."

"Shh, boy, shh!" Will whispered as he helped Duffy out of the thoroughly soaked clothing.

Hannah caught the bottles of milk just before they would have fallen to the floor. Willy was screaming with hunger which made it hard to hear and understand Duffy.

"Sit down and eat ye some mush whilst I warm this bottle for yer big-mouthed brother."

Duffy was suddenly ravenous, and devoured two bowls of mush without a breath. When Hannah finally had Willy resting quietly in her arms in the rocker before the kitchen fire, Duffy turned tear-filled eyes to them.

"It's horrid out there. It's like a terrible nightmare. You can't see and the wind howls so nasty-like. And, oh, Mama, . . . Papa . . . I must not have latched the shutters on the barn window tight. Or else the wind broke 'em somehow. The window was open . . . and . . . and the goats are gone."

"Never you mind, son. 'twasn't anything yer fault." Will gently rubbed Duffy's shoulders as he spoke. "There's nothin' we can do until the storm eases a little.

44

Get yerself into all dry, warm clothing, from the skin out, Duffy. This crazy weather has to let up soon. Mayhap by this afternoon we can go look for the goats. Meantime, you get warm whilst I go feed the horses."

Duffy looked confused. "But, I did, Papa. I did all the barn chorin'."

As the boy walked out of the room, Will turned adoring eyes on Hannah. "My lady, how'd we raise us such a fine son? As beattled as he must have been by the storm, I ne'er dreamed he would remember to care for the animals. And to bring in milk for Willy, too. He's sure somethin'."

Hannah nodded her agreement as a sleepy-eyed Libby entered the room. "I'm hungry," she exclaimed. "I must've slept late if Willy's been fed already. What's that funny sing-songy noise?"

" 'Tis a horrible wind, Miss Liberty," Hannah said as she shoved a bowl of warm mush in front of her daughter. "Eat hearty."

Pulling Will through the pantry door away from Libby's worrisome ears, she voiced her fear in a whisper. "What will we do about the goats?"

Chapter 8

he storm raged on all day and into the night. Used to the normally fair weather of Norfolk, the Stivers family like all their neighbors suffered from cabin fever. All through the long day, Hannah tried to keep the children busy. She had set Libby down with quilt squares before her on the large kitchen table with an order to sew them together. Duffy was working on memorizing the times tables, an assignment his wise teacher had determined would take most of the Christmas vacation from school. Hannah's biggest problem was Will. He paced the floor, sat down to read or whittle for a spell, then got up to pace the floor again. Every hour or so he would open the kitchen door, then slam it shut with a remark like, " 'Tisn't fit for man nor beast to be out. Can't go lookin' yet, Duffy. Alls that'd happen would be we'd get ourselves lost, and what'd that gain us?" Everyone's nerves grew taut. Late in the afternoon, after a supper of vegetables from the root cellar as it grew dark, Will opened the door again.

Hannah exploded. "Will, please. Quit openin' the door and lettin' all the cold air rush in! You can tell by lookin' out the window that the storm hasn't lessened any."

The children stared at their mother. Hannah so rarely raised her voice that it startled them to utter silence.

At precisely that moment Willy awoke in his cradle by the fireplace and screamed for all he was worth. Libby rushed to soothe the baby while Hannah collapsed in her daughter's former seat. She leaned her head on her crossed arms on the table and began to sob.

"My lady, what is it?" Will asked as he rubbed her shoulders.

"I gave him the the last bottle. What can I give poor Willy to eat?"

Duffy was on his feet pulling on his coat instantly. "Don't worry, Mama. There was more goats' milk in the springhouse. I'll fetch it."

Hannah's relief was evident on her still tear-stained face. "How much is there, son?"

"A bucketful, with oilcloth over the top was sittin' in the spring," Duffy responded.

"Wait, son," Will said as he too began to don warmer clothing. "I think this is a two-man job. Whilst we're out we may as well tend to the barn chorin'. But here, let's take this rope from the pantry and make us a guide to hang onto in this storm."

And so Will and Duffy battled their way through nearly waist-high drifts to get to the barn and springhouse. As they came to every tree, Will secured the rope around it so that on their journey back, walking directly into the wind, they'd have a hand hold. They gave the horses fresh hay and rubbed them down with vigor. They broke the ice on their troughs and all the animals immediately drank their fill.

As Duffy had predicted, there was just one small bucketful of the precious goats' milk in the springhouse. Somehow they managed to get it inside without spilling a great amount. Though they'd only been out in the storm a short time, it had taken its toll. Both Will and his son stood panting, dripping snow and ice all over the hooked rug by the door.

Hannah thought she'd never been so glad and relieved to see anything as the bucket of milk, for Willy had never stopped screaming during his brother and father's trip out in the storm. She grabbed the bucket and plunged the glass bottle in the milk to fill it. Then she placed the bottle in a pan of water on the stove to warm it.

During this entire scenario, Libby paced the floor carrying Willy, patting his back, saying, "There, there little brother." The baby screamed on. Will and Duffy took off their wet duds and stood before the fire trying to regain feeling in their frozen extremities. Eventually, Hannah took the baby and the urgent wails were replaced by grateful sucking noises.

"Oh, Duffy," his mother sighed, "I don't know what we'd a done if ya hadn't remembered the bucket of milk. Thank you, son."

Duffy ducked his head in embarrassment. Hannah turned to her husband. "Has the storm slackened any?" His discouraged shake of the head was her only reply.

"What'll we do about the goats, Papa?" Libby asked.

"I'm just not knowin' for sure, Lib—but one thing we're not goin' ta do is worry 'bout 'em. They've got sense enough to find some kind of shelter from the storm." Turning his attention toward Hannah, Will went on. "Seems to me a perfect time to play the thankful game. What do you say, my lady?"

A collective sigh of relief escaped the lips of all present. The thankful game was something which took them all back in their memories. Will and Hannah had instructed the children in the rules of the game from the time they could talk.

" 'Tis simple, really," they would say. "The Bible

says that we are to give thanks in everything. To rejoice evermore. So we'll just go 'round our family circle with each namin' somethin' they're thankful for." When Duffy and Libby were smaller, the game had been short. For they had only been able to think of a few things to name. But now that they were older their understanding went deeper, and the game was a way to get their minds off present problems. Though everyone understood this, it continued to work well.

"I'll go first," piped Libby after they pulled chairs into a circle before the fire. "I'm thankful that Duffy knew about that one last bucket of goats' milk 'cause I don't think I could have stood one more second of Willy's screaming." Everyone nodded and grinned.

Next Hannah spoke. She looked at the baby in her arms as she spoke. "Well, though this one's screaming for his bottle had me nigh crazy a bit ago, I guess I'm thankful that he *can* scream and cry like that. 'Twasn't so long ago we thought he never would."

Duffy was next to Hannah. He hesitated, then spoke softly. "Well, I guess it's the obvious answer today. But I'm thankful for the home we have and that we don't have to be outside in that ... that ..." A visible shudder shook his body as he gave up trying to find the right word.

Will patted his son on the shoulder. "I've got one that'll surprise all of ya. Believe it or not, I'm thankin' God today *for* the snow!" His whole family turned confused faces toward him. He continued. "We needed it. The winter wheat I planted would never have seen the light of day without some kind of moisture. So I've been a prayin' for some rain or snow. Well, the Lord certainly did see fit to answer that prayer!"

Laughter filled the little kitchen as once again the Stivers family learned that thankfulness is the best antidote to worry.

"My turn again," said Libby. She looked at her

mother with pleading eyes and a mischievous grin as she spoke. "I'm thankful to God that we have some nice popcorn in the bin in the pantry because it sure would taste good."

"Oh, Libby, you are a swindler for sure! But, yes, go ahead," Hannah grinned.

The girl danced across the room and got a cup of the corn which she placed in the long-handled popper. "Don't stop the game, though. We'll just have to talk louder when it starts to pop," she said as she knelt before the fire and began to shake the popper over the flame. "C'mon, Mama. It's your turn."

"Well, I'm thankful that the good Lord saw fit to let us have that chance meeting with my cousin, Katrina. Though we were never very close, I've oft wondered about my family back in Germany. It makes me sad to to think of them all bein' dead and gone, but still I'm thankful that I know. 'Twas the not knowin' that was hard." As usual, this game brought to light some feelings that the family never would have known about in any other way.

"It appears I'm gonna have to shout my answer," grinned Duffy as the corn began to pop merrily. "I guess I'm thankful for the fact that the window in the barn isn't big enough for any of the other animals to have gotten out in the storm except the stupid goats."

Will's glance across the top of Duffy's head told Hannah he was worried about the boy's state of mind. She gave her son a playful pat on the back.

"C'mon, Duff, get your heart in the game and off worryin' 'bout the storm. Whyn't you fetch some cider from the root cellar? Sounds as if the popcorn's nearly done."

And so there was a break in the game as Duffy lifted the floor-board door in the pantry and descended the short ladder to the cellar. Soon everyone was settled before the fire again holding large bowls of the lightly salted popcorn and mugs of sweet cider.

"Whose turn is it?" Libby asked.

I believe it's mine," Will said. "And I'm like your Mama. I, too, am thankful for Katrina's visit because hopefully it will bring about another visit . . . a lifelong visit from your grandmother, children." He had a far-away look in his eyes.

"What is she like, Papa?" asked Duffy. And because it was the first time the boy's mind had been off the storm, or perhaps because the timing seemed just right, Will decided to answer his son rather than go on with the game.

"Hmmm . . . it is hard to put into words what Mother is like." He chuckled. "That word *Mother* sort of gives you a clue. We never would have dared to call her Mama. She is very . . . how can I say it? She's very *proper* all the time. She holds herself very straight and tall and I oft got the impression as a lad that she practiced through in her mind everything she ever said before she said it out loud. She speaks very quietly, but at least at Stivers' Castle, whatever she says is the law."

Libby interrupted. "She doesn't sound like a very fun person to be around."

Hannah was going to scold Libby for her outburst but Will intervened.

"Well, Miss Liberty, though one hates to admit it, I'm afraid you're right. She almost always had a little smile on her face, but it kind of looked like it was painted on, not a real smile. It's odd . . . I can only remember ever hearing her laugh . . . I mean *really* laugh . . . one time. A family had come to visit us at the castle. This family lived in one of the big cities of Germany and had never been out in the country before. There was a boy about my age who said he wanted to explore the barns with me. He was making fun of our way of life, trying to make me feel odd because we lived in the country, even though it was a castle we lived in. So I thought I'd teach him a lesson. He wanted to know what we did for fun, and I told him we dove into piles of hay from the loft of the barn. We had a jolly day, jumping and rolling and sliding down what he thought was a big pile of hay. But 'twas really a huge stack of manure awaiting to be spread on the fields."

Libby and Duffy were beside themselves with glee. To think of their papa as an ornery little boy teaching a city slicker a lesson. It was grand.

"Oh, Will, you didn't!" exclaimed Hannah wiping tears of laughter and still shaking with giggles. "What did your mother do?"

"Well," Will resumed the narrative, "that's what I could never really understand. She was always so . . . so . . . prim and proper in every way. I expected the scolding of my life. I left the boy still in the barn, snuck back into the castle and got myself all cleaned up. I gave my clothing to the maid who disposed of it discreetly. So when we were called for dinner, only the other boy was in, shall we say, a royal disarray. When questioned, he said, "Master William and I were playing in the hay." My mother literally burst into laughter. Father was appalled and punished me severely. Later I heard him lecturing her on our station in life, and he must have been quite severe, for I never heard her laugh again."

By now the popcorn was gone. Libby had carried the dishes to the dry sink where they would wait to be washed with the breakfast things. She put her arm around Hannah.

"I'm glad our own Mama laughs a lot."

Hannah spoke. "Sounds as if your mother is to be pitied, Will. Mayhap the atmosphere of the castle and always having to remember to live up to being the wife of a Lord took a happy woman and totally stifled her. You were never happy there. Mayhap when she comes to America, she will learn to be happy like you have."

Will nodded thoughtfully. Then he brightened. "Whose turn is it? I've lost track."

Libby laughed. "I said I'm glad Mama laughs, but now I'll make it officially a part of the game. I'm thankful for laughter."

Hannah said, "That makes it my turn. And I'm thankful that soon we shall meet Grandmother Stivers and mayhap teach her to laugh with us."

Duffy had remained pretty quiet through much of the evening. "I can't think of anything," he mumbled.

"Oh, come now, son. We've so much to be thankful for," his father corrected.

"All right all right," the boy replied grumpily. "Then I'm thankful that at least there's enough milk in the bucket to give Willy his middle of the night feeding. But I don't know what we'll do come . . ."

Will interrupted and ended the game as he always did. Even the worried Duffy had to smile as Papa said, "I'm thankful for America and all this blessed country stands for—especially . . ."

Here Will waited until the family joined him and sing-songed in unison, "especially Freedom, Liberty, and Justice!" They all understood that Papa was thankful both for the reality of those qualities of life here in America, but also for his children whom he had given those names.

Libby stifled a yawn and Mama said, "It's bedtime. Each of you children take those rocks warming at the edge of the fire and rush on up to bed. If ya hurry, they'll warm yer feet till ya fall asleep."

After hugs and kisses all around, Will banked the fire for the evening and everyone went to bed. Outside, the wind howled as the storm raged on.

Chapter 9

or a few minutes Duffy could not decide what had wakened him. Then he heard muted cries from Willy downstairs in Mama and Papa's room. "Oh, 'tis just little brother's middle of the night feeding," he mumbled to himself as he rolled over and pulled the covers up tight. But then he remembered with a sick heart, 'twas the last bottle available. Sitting up in bed he realized too how totally silent it was. Complete quiet. No howling wind.

Pulling the warm covers with him and wrapping himself like a cocoon, Duffy tiptoed to his window. The shutters on the outside were closed, but with a few taps the ice gave way and Duffy threw open the window. What he saw nearly took his breath away. The moon was full and as golden as the sun at noonday. Below, the world was a glorious golden, silver and white wonderland. It was extremely quiet. Duffy felt almost as if he had entered a cathedral. The scene below his window was holy. No snow fell. No movement was caused by wind. He stood and stared in amazement.

Suddenly his peripheral vision caught some movement off to the right. At the edge of the barn stood a beautiful deer. She stood still for several minutes, only her nose twitching. Then for no apparent reason she bounded out across the fields. A sigh escaped Duffy's lips at her beauty. He watched the white tail bounding far off until she entered the woods and was out of sight.

The movement of the deer seemed to energize Duffy. Leaving the shutters open for light, he silently threw off the covers and began to dress. "If the deer are movin' about, the stupid goats can too," he whispered to himself as he hurriedly dressed in many warm layers of clothing. Carrying his shoes and boots, he tiptoed down the stairs, past Mama and Papa's room and into the kitchen. His slate was still where he had left it as he did multiplication tables earlier, so he erased it and quickly printed, "Storm is over—Bright moon—Gone to find goats. Love, Duffy"

Stepping outside, he breathed a sigh of relief at not being caught. Whispering, "Lord, please guide me directly to the goats," he plunged off into the snow.

Perhaps it was because the day before had been so nerve-wracking. Perhaps it was because the howling wind had finally ceased. Perhaps because unexplainedly Willy slept peacefully. Whatever the reason, Will and Hannah and Libby slept on and on. Will, who was always up at dawn, was absolutely appalled to find the sun well up in an azure sky when he first opened his eyes. Allowing Hannah to sleep on, he threw more wood on the fire and hung a pot of coffee over it. Then he went to the barn for chores. He was thankful for the rope to hold onto. He no longer needed it because of visibility but, because of the depth of the snow, it aided in walking. He was just finishing up in the barn when he heard shouts from the house.

"Will! Will, where are you? Please, come quickly!"

Detecting terror in his wife's voice, Will immediately plunged back to the house, nearly falling with every running step. Halfway there he saw Hannah standing

55

on the back porch in only her thin robe, her long hair streaming down around her shoulders. "Will," she cried between sobs, "Hurry!"

"My lady, what is it?"

"It's Duffy! He's gone!" she sobbed as he finally gained the porch and pushed her inside.

She held up the slate which Will had overlooked in his rush to get to the chores. "I knew he felt responsible. He always worries so about Willy. I should've expected ..." she broke into sobs again. "What'll we do? Where'll we look?"

Will took hold of Hannah's shoulders and gently took control of the situation. "Hannah, get ahold of yourself. We must not panic. Duffy is a big boy and he can take care of himself. He won't do anything foolish. You mustn't be crying when Libby comes down else she will be uncontrollable. Now, you get a warm breakfast going. I'll change into warmer dry clothes, drink some coffee, and then I'll start searching. Shouldn't be hard to follow his tracks iffen the storm had already stopped when he left."

Hannah knew her husband was right, so she busied herself making oatmeal, and praying the whole time for the safety of her firstborn.

Libby stumbled into the kitchen asking, "What time is it?" almost on the heels of a completely bundled Will. He devoured a bowl of the oatmeal and had just set his cup of coffee down when everyone turned at the unexpected sound of bells in the front yard.

"What on earth?" Hannah muttered as Libby raced for the door.

"It's Little Marc ... in a sleigh ... and he's got animals ... our goats! And Duffy!" she exclaimed.

By this time all were on the porch, Hannah still heedless of the cold. Little Marc Woodcutter was helping Duffy down out of his father's big sleigh. Duffy was wrapped in what Hannah recognized as some of

56

Lucille's best blankets. He wore a coat no one recognized and could barely walk, from fatigue or the overabundance of coverings no one could tell. He shook with chills and his cheeks were crimson with fever. His eyes were bright, though, and he managed a smile as he said, "They're all right. We left Jonah at Uncle Marc's 'cause he seemed kind of wobbly and weak . . . but we brought the others home."

Hannah had both arms around Duffy with tears streaming down her face as she helped him remove the cumbersome blankets. He put one foot on the stairs, but she guided him to the kitchen daybed instead. She handed him a mug of strong coffee and said, "Don't talk. Drink."

Will and Little Marc had busied themselves getting Henrietta, Harriet, and Herbert tethered, fed, and milked in the barn. By the time they entered the kitchen, Libby was eating oatmeal, Hannah was changing Willy's diaper, and Duffy was almost asleep. Hannah ordered them all to the sitting room to allow Duffy to rest, and she gave Willy his freshly warmed bottle. It was then they finally learned a little of Duffy's story.

Little Marc spoke quietly so as not to disturb his sleeping friend. " 'Twas just first light when we heard a commotion on the back porch. We couldn't believe anyone would be up and about as deep as the snow was. But Samantha came up the stairs a hollerin' something awful."

"It's Masta Freedom," she said, "and I think he's 'bout froze to deaf!"

"Well, you know Mama. She about went into a fit and made poor Duff strip to the skin. Her and Samantha rubbed his whole body down with snow, him crying and begging them to stop. I never saw skin so red in my life. Don't know if he was that embarrassed or if he's frostbit head to toe."

Will interrupted. "Whichever, your mama did the

right thing. He may not lose any of his body to frostbite iffen they got to him fast enough."

Little Marc continued. "He was talking all the time about the goats. Went on and on about how it was his fault they got out and how he'd snuck out to find them. He didn't have any idea where to look but he said he kept prayin' and finally he remembered a real tight thicket right by the stream in our woods and he just thought they might a' gone in there for shelter. So he went there and sure enough, that's where they were. Sure is a good thing the moon was so bright last night so's he could see. Samantha said when he fell onto the porch he was holding the kid, Jonah, in his arms and he wouldn't let go of him. By the way, Uncle Will, Papa would have driven him home in the sleigh, but he was a workin' with Jonah. He's awful froze up. I don't know if he'll make it or not."

"Poor Jonah," Libby whispered. "But at least Duffy is all right, isn't he?"

"Well, Mama did her best with him," said Little Marc. "After the rubbing they gave him with snow they wrapped him in blankets I held to the fire to heat. She made him put on two layers of my clothes and then drink hot brandy and tea. She said she was going to put him to bed but he screamed,, "No! Willy needs the milk!" So she said rather than to rile him any further I should race him home in the sleigh. She knew you folks'd be worried sick!"

"How will I ever thank Lucille?" Hannah asked.

"Oh, Aunt Hannah, somehow Mama knew you'd say that. She said if you did, I was to say whatever she did was simply paying back a debt she's owed you from a Christmas a long time ago." The boy looked confused, but Hannah nodded, remembering.

Hannah worried over Duffy and wouldn't even allow him out of bed for the next three days, but other than a nasty cold he was none the worse for wear from his night in the woods. By the time Hannah allowed Duffy up, all the remnants of the storm were gone and spring was in the air. The snow which had blanketed everything had gone away, leaving mud in its place. Out near the barn the goats, including a recovered Jonah, romped merrily. When Duffy finally received permission to go outside, Will walked with him to the nearest field. They laughed as Will removed the now unnecessary rope guide from the house to the barn. Just beyond the barn, Will pointed to the field.

"See. The snow accomplished its purpose." Duffy smiled as he saw the entire field was covered with wheat already showing its green heads.

* * * * * * * * * * *

Spring raced through the land that year touching everything in its path. Almost immediately upon the disappearance of the snow, the air grew warm and the atmosphere smelled earthy. Within a few weeks the ladies of the Norfolk area were trying to out-do each other with cleaning. Carpets were hung over lines and beaten while inside everything smelled of strong lye soap.

Hannah was no exception to the rule. Only her ministrations were a bit more frenzied than ever before as she tried to prepare her house and herself for the imminent arrival of Will's mother.

A wall had hastily been thrown up through Libby's room. The girl was more than willing to sacrifice the space as she'd always been a bit frightened in her large room anyway. She looked forward to having a new Grandmother just on the other side of that wall.

They attended a sale of household goods the third week of February. The Longport family was selling nearly everything they owned and heading west. Hannah thought her luck was beyond belief when she was able to purchase a lovely three piece bedroom suite, complete with a good mattress, out of her small savings. After a thorough cleaning and a careful placement of the lovely mahogany furniture, the new room, now known as Grandmother's room, was ready. It would sit thus, untouched, except for a weekly cleaning and airing, for several more weeks.

Chapter 10

ooking back, Hannah often wondered if the family could have stood the excitement of waiting for Grandmother's arrival, had not another event come about to distract them.

Little Marc Woodcutter was soon to turn sixteen years old. His birthday would be on March thirty-first. Normally a family celebration sufficed the children of the area, but this would be the last birthday Little Marc would celebrate at home. He was registered to attend William and Mary College in the city of Williamsburg in the fall. His sisters, Karla and Louisa Witherspoon, talked their mother into throwing a grand party.

" 'Twill be the most gala celebration this town has e'er seen," said Karla as the ladies all quilted together. "Mama, if only our house was bigger, I'd want to have the party right here. 'Twill be such an exciting evening."

"Too grand and too exciting, if you ask me," grumbled Mistress Woodcutter. "I only hope all this high-fallutin' tomfoolery don't go to Little Marc's head."

"Oh, Mama, don't throw a wet blanket on our fun!"

urged Louisa. "It's been a long time since there's been a party of any kind. And we really ought to do something special for Little Marc. He's always been such a blessing to the family."

"He is that, I'll not deny it," said their mother as she sat staring off through the window. "I wish it wasn't so far to Williamsburg. I know he's learned all he can here at our school, but, oh! How I shall miss him!" Her eyes were filled with tears.

"Ladies, ladies," Hannah giggled. "If we don't get to quilting, we never shall get this finished. The log cabin is such a tedious pattern to quilt, don't you think?"

All the ladies turned their hands back to the task at hand, but their minds were still on the approaching soiree.

"Is there any way I can help with the party, Lucille?" Hannah asked.

"Well, no ... thank you anyway, dear. Naturally Samantha has taken over all the food planning. And the cleaning can't be done too far in advance else we'd just have to do it all twice. Karla, did you speak with that man about the orchestra?"

Karla grinned. "It's not a whole orchestra, Mama. Just a string quartet. Yes, it's all arranged. They said they do mostly minuets and waltzes though I did insist we shall want some square dances and reels."

"Oh, my," Hannah interrupted. "It *shall* be something grand. I hadn't realized there was to be dancing."

Lucille laughed nervously. "It's all these girls' doing. They had to do some mighty fast talking to talk their brother into the idea of a dinner dance."

Louisa spoke up. "Well, he'll just have to get used to the idea. Any boy as handsome as he's becoming should be required to pay some attention to the neighborhood girls. Why you can see it in their eyes at church on Sundays. They'd all just nearly die if he would so much as glance their direction. So, if dancing will get him to begin to think about girls, it will be worth it."

Karla giggled. "Mama, I don't think you realize that the young man living under your roof is thought to be the prize catch of all. Why, the other day I overheard Marta and a group of her friends talking and they all think there's no one quite like Little Marc. And the last sentence I heard nearly choked me. Marta was talking and she said, "Well, girls—just you mind—if it weren't for the fact that he's my uncle, none of you would stand a chance with Little Marc 'cause I'd never stop until I got a proposal out of him!"

The ladies all laughed as they continued to quilt. Good friends took the tedium out of the job. Needles flew through the fabric, and friendships were bound together as tightly as the top, batting, and backing of the quilt.

Still thinking about the party, Louisa changed the subject to one more pressing. "I don't know how I shall ever get the sewing all done. My Hannah chose a pattern for her party dress with the entire bodice smocked. I've never been good at smocking anyway, but she wants it so badly."

"I'll be glad to help you with it, dear. It's been a long time since I've done any smocking, but I'm pretty sure I remember how," her mother said.

"Oh, Mama, could you? But no . . . I'm sure you're too busy with your own things."

"Nonsense," replied Lucille. "I shall wear my watered silk from last year. Marc offered me a new dress, but I really don't need it. Little Marc won't be paying any attention to me anyway. 'Twill be a young people's party. I've no sewing whatsoever to do, for Little Marc is to have his first tailor-made suit. Marc took him into Norfolk yesterday for his first fitting." Turning her attention elsewhere, she continued. "What about you, Hannah? Will you have a new dress?"

"Nay, not for me," Hannah replied. "But Libby is driving me wild. Will thinks it is too soon for her to have another new dress since Christmas. But, in truth, the child is outgrowing everything she owns. Will finally gave in last evening and said she may have a new party dress, and I thought that would settle it. But nay, we spent the rest of the evening discussing this dress—*how* it shall be made, *of what* it shall be made, but, oh, the most important thing of all. She turned those huge eyes on me and said, "Oh, Mama . . . more than *anything else*, it must make me look grown-up. Please, please, Mama. It must be an adult pattern and make me look as old as the other girls (meaning Hannah and Marta, I presume). And oh, Mama, do you think it could be *long?*" I tell you, it's scary how Libby is growing up. She's throwin' away all the carefree days of her childhood a-wishin' she was older.'"

Karla had been thoughtful during Hannah's long narrative. "Well, Hannah, she is nigh a young lady. I noticed the other day how grown-up she has become in the last few months. How old is she now?"

"She turned twelve last month," Hannah answered.

"She looks and acts much older than that. I think if I were you, I'd let her drop her skirts and put her hair up. Some children just mature faster than others. Why, Chad and I were married when I was only one year older than Libby."

Heads shook all around the quilt as others put in their thoughts on the issue. Hannah finally settled the matter by saying, "Well, I think Lib's party dress will be as long as the older girls, but mainly just so it will fit longer—not because we're going to let her grow up that fast. And her hair shall be down, I think. Why, she's just a little girl after all."

If Little Marc had comprehended half the hubbub this party was stirring up in the female half of the populace, he probably would have cancelled the whole

64

thing. While the ladies' quilting bee took place at his sister Karla's, he and Duffy were fishing.

"So, what are we gonna do at this big party of yours, Marc?"

"Aw, I don't know. I wish they'd just leave it alone like your folks did when you turned fourteen. But I guess Karla and Louisa want to have this big shindig since I'm going off to school."

"Are ya lookin' forward to goin' to William and Mary?"

"Well, Duff—it's hard to say. In some ways I am and in some ways I'm not. I'll sure miss you!"

"Yeah, but just think of all the new things you'll be seein' and doin'. I envy you," Duffy said, trying to ignore the lump he got in his throat whenever he thought of Little Marc going away. "Sometimes I get so sick of livin' in the same place, doin' the same things all the time. Pa said last night when we were chorin' in the barn that he thinks I've got ramblin' blood in my veins, like him."

"Maybe you'll come to William and Mary and join me in a couple of years, eh?" Little Marc asked.

"Not me! I don't wanna be no preacher!"

"Well, neither do I!"

"Then why are you goin' to William and Mary? I thought everyone who went there became preachers!"

"They do! But not me. I'm going to be a lawyer someday."

"A lawyer? Why, you could learn to do that just by apprenticing yourself to that fella here in town that always wears that powdered wig. Why're ya goin' clear up there to William and Mary?"

"It's hard to explain, Duff. But my head seems like a sponge a wanting to soak up all the learning it can. So I'm going to study all that theology and Latin and everything I can. It'll probably help me to argue cases in court. But then I'll study with one of the men in

Williamsburg and maybe someday, I'll be in the House of Burgesses!"

Not to be out-done by his friend, Duffy said, "Well, for me, I'll just be glad to be shut of schooling for good after this year. And I might be getting away from Norfolk just the same as you some day."

Little Marc tried to hide his shock. "Whatever are you talking about, Duffy?"

Duffy self-consciously glanced all around and lowered his voice, though he knew that he and his friend were the only humans for miles. "Well, you got to promise not to tell."

Both boys grinned as Little Marc proceeded with their childhood promise sign, a crossed heart, two hand slaps, and spit over his left shoulder.

"Well, out with it, Duff. What's the secret?" urged Marc.

"It's not for sure, yet. And mayhap won't be for a long time. But I think eventually our family's goin' ta move."

"Move? But where?"

"West . . . and north some, I think. Seems Pa overheard men talkin' in the general store. Some man by the name of Boone was trying to interest people in movin' to the Kentucky territory. It's a long fearsome trail to get there, but once you are there they say there's beautiful farmin' land as far as the eye can see. And it's nigh onto totally unsettled." Duffy's eyes seemed lit from within as he spoke.

"But aren't you scared of Indians?" asked his older companion.

"Pa says nothin' is as fearsome as bein' crowded in on all sides like we are now. He's been upset ever since that Martin clan began breakin' the soil on that piece to our west. Says he don't feel free anymore!"

"What about yer Ma?" asked Little Marc trying to regain his composure after the shock of the very idea of losing his best friend to a move.

"Well, that's why it's a secret. Don't say anything to your folks until I say. 'Cause I'm not even supposed to know. I overheard them talkin' several nights in a row. You know the fireplace in my room directly connects to the one in theirs. Well, Pa just kept talking up all the virtues of movin' west. He's even heard of a place farther away than Kentucky called Ohio. It's supposed to have land so flat you don't even have to shoe your horses to plow it. But Ma sure isn't keen on the idea of movin'. She talks a lot about not wantin' to leave yer Ma and Pa, nor the house, nor nothing. Well Pa . . . he kinda gave it up. But then night before last I heard her say, 'Will, I know that you've got yer heart set on movin' west. And so I'm a tellin' ya this to give ya some hope. I'm thinkin' and prayin' about it.' "

"What did yer Pa say then?"

"Well, it got all quiet for a while. I suppose they was kissing like they always do, you know. And then he said, 'Thank you, Hannah. Iffen you'll just think and pray about it, that's all a man can ask. But I'll promise you, my lady . . . we'll not e'er move unless we're agreed.' "

"Do they know you can hear them from yer room?" Marc whispered in awe.

"Well, they didn't! But I told Pa I overheard them and I want to move, too. He got real stern and said I shouldn't listen to their private conversations. But he also said I should hope and pray Mama will see the light so's we can move."

All was quiet for several minutes as each boy pursued his own thoughts while watching for the bobbing of a cork.

"What do you suppose it feels like?" Little Marc asked suddenly.

"What what feels like?" Duffy responded.

"You know . . . kissing a girl!"

Duffy couldn't have been more surprised. Evidently Little Marc's mind was back on their conversation about Mama and Papa.

"Why on earth would you wonder that?" exploded Duffy. "It makes me feel sick to even think of it."

"Not me!" responded his older friend. "I've been wondering a lot about it lately ... and I just might decide to give it a try at this stupid birthday party. I mean, if we're gonna have to dance with them we may as well try some of the other stuff too!"

Duffy stared at his friend with his mouth hanging open. What on earth was happening to Little Marc? Suddenly he didn't even care to attend this fancy birthday party for his friend.

The day finally arrived and girls and boys between the ages of ten and sixteen all over the area made themselves ready for the party. As the sun began to set in the western sky, the long circular driveway to the Woodcutter's home was filled with carriages, buggies, and light wagons bringing children to help Little Marc turn sixteen.

Immediately upon arrival they were ushered into the dining room. Will and Hannah were the only other adult chaperones besides the Woodcutters and Witherspoons. As they entered the dining room, Hannah was reminded of her first night in America. The silver shone in the same way. Many of the dishes were the same, but Samantha had truly out-done herself with this meal. There was roast beef, a giant ham dotted with cloves, and a sumptuous turkey. One huge bowl held mashed potatoes, another boasted sweet potatoes, and still a third had escalloped potatoes. There was stuffing with the turkey. Every garden vegetable imaginable was on the table, as well as corn bread, light bread, and even sugar scones. It was a feast fit for a king to be sure, and Little Marc seemed to be enjoying his role as king. The girls scarcely ate at all, for many of them were laced into corsets which gave them eighteen-inch waists but allowed little room for breathing. But the boys put a large dent in the food. When all seemed satisfied, the servants cleared the table. All grew quiet as Samantha entered the far door of the room carrying a birthday cake which surely must have been designed in heaven. In unison the party-goers "aahed" at her creation, and Samantha glowed. As she set the cake in front of Little March with all sixteen candles reflecting in her eyes, she gave him a quick peck on the cheek. Will's deep bass voice began the traditional birthday song and as the chorus receded Little Marc stood to his feet. With one great breath, he extinguished the candles to a round of applause. After cake was enjoyed by all, the party moved across the hall to the drawing room. Carpets had been rolled up, the stringed instruments were tuned, and the room soon became a ballroom. The first dance was awkward due to the youth of the party-goers, but once Little Marc and his niece Marta took the floor they were joined by others. Soon a lively reel broke out, and it seemed more like games than serious dancing.

"It appears the girls have all tried to out-do each other, doesn't it?" Hannah asked Will.

"There's none any lovelier than Lib," he responded. "But she looks so unhappy. Iffen I knew how to dance, I'd get her out on that floor."

Hannah turned sad eyes on her daughter. Libby stood with a group of her school chums. They all looked lovely in new dresses and professional coiffures. But Hannah had to agree with Will. Even with her hair hanging in loose curls around her shoulders, Libby was the loveliest of all. But the girl appeared to be on the verge of tears.

Suddenly, as if a lamp had been lit in her mind, Hannah understood. For just then Little Marc waltzed by with a girl Hannah didn't know on his arm. Libby's heart was in her eyes as they followed him around the room.

"Why, I declare!" Hannah whispered to herself. "Our little girl loves him too!"

Excusing herself from Will, Hannah maneuvered herself around the floor to where Duffy and some boys stood chatting about school.

"Duffy," she whispered, "do me a favor."

The next dance was going to be a square dance. As the guests broke into groups of four couples, Hannah saw the first smile of the evening on Libby's lips as she paired with her brother in the same square with Little Marc.

"Well, a dance with a brother is better than no dance at all . . . right, my lady?"

Hannah blushed, wondering if others beside her husband were able to see through her subterfuge.

Libby's smiles remained only through the one dance. Then she rejoined the younger girls who weren't dancing. Once she realized how unhappy Libby was, Hannah wished the evening would come to an early end. But it seemed to drag on. Just when she thought she could bear it no longer, the front door of the home opened with a surprise no one expected for Little Marc's birthday.

"So, Marcus Phillip, how does it feel to be sixteen years old?" boomed the unexpected guest. "And Will . . . Will Stivers . . . ye best head fer home post haste. Yer mama insisted that I leave her there!" Captain Phillip Woodcutter had returned.

Chapter 11

fter hasty goodbyes all around, the Stivers family piled into their buggy. Will and Duffy were up on the driver's seat. Thankfully, Willy never awoke as he was brought to Hannah by one of the servants, so she could turn all her attention to this woman-child who needed her desperately.

"Oh, Mama," Libby exploded, her body shaking with sobs. "Why did I ever think he would care about my new dress? Why did I think he would even look at me?"

Hannah did not have any idea of how to comfort Libby. She put her arm around her and drew the shaking body over against her shoulder.

"There, there Lib. Don't take on so. It was only a birthday party. And you looked so lovely and grown up," she added.

"No, no, I didn't. He didn't think I looked grown up. He'll always think of me as his playmate, as Duffy's little sister. He never even spoke to me except to say 'Hi, kid' when he was on his way to get punch for that town girl, Emily Gibson. He danced with her over and over again. But he never even looked at me!" She sobbed uncontrollably again.

"Oh, honey lamb, I wish I could take away all the horrid pain you're feeling right now. I never dreamed that you had a special caring for Little Marc."

Libby was so upset she did not even realize that her long-guarded secret was out. "A special caring? Mama, I've loved Little Marc Woodcutter for as long as I can remember. But I can't ever love him again. Not after tonight. In fact, I'm never goin' to love any boy as long as I live." Each outburst brought more tears.

"Never say never, Libby. Never is a long, long time," the wise mother counselled.

Now the girl just cried quietly, shaking her head every so often as if to say that she just couldn't believe her wonderful Little Marc could have treated her so cruelly. Though Hannah's heart ached for Libby, she had to turn her thoughts to the more pressing issue—that of meeting her mother-in-law.

"Libby," she said, "you must get control of yourself. Look, we are almost home. And your new Grandmother is going to be waiting there. Here, dry your eyes and try to stop crying. Please, dear—for me! I do want so desperately for all of us to make a favorable impression on her."

"I'll try, Mama," Libby mumbled, but continued to cry quietly.

Hannah was in such turmoil on the inside she wondered for a brief moment if she was going to be sick. "No," she thought. "I'll not allow my nerves to get control of me. After all, it's only Will's mother. She loves Will and I love Will and surely we shall be able to get along well." But then worry reared its ugly head and nearly took over Hannah's mind. "Why didn't I air and clean her room today? What will she think of our humble little home after living in that castle? She'll be hungry. What can I possibly feed her? Oh dear, her first impression of Libby is going to be a horrid one." Such thoughts might have gone unchecked the rest of the way home had not another word from Libby brought her mind back to reality. The girl was still crying, but mumbling something under her breath.

"What's that, Lib? what did you say?"

"Oh, nothing, Mama. I just can't seem to quit crying. So I was remembering what teacher said last week when he put our memory verse up."

"What's that, dear?"

"It's from the book of Philippians," Libby choked out. "It says ... *I can* ... *I can do all things through* ... *through Christ who strengtheneth me.* I just hope I can stop crying."

Once again, as happened so often, Hannah was amazed at how one of her children could nearly confound her with a deep spiritual truth.

"Libby, let's pray," Hannah said. The two ladies bowed their heads and held hands while Willy slept peacefully on Hannah's other arm.

"Dear Lord," Hannah began, "you know all about everything that's happened tonight. You know how sad and upset our Libby is. And Lord, I pray you will wrap your big arms of love around her and help her to quit crying. Lord, you also know how I'm feelin' about meetin' Will's mother. Please help me to face whatever is ahead and help us all to show her love. God, help both me and Lib to remember that we can do all things through the strength of your Son in whose Name we pray. Amen."

Libby gave Hannah a wobbly smile as she added her Amen. Just then the buggy stopped and Duffy shouted, "We're home."

Before Hannah could even open the buggy door, Will was on the porch and entering the house yelling, "Mother! Mother, where are you?"

For just an instant, Hannah felt jealous. Will *always* helped her down from the buggy. And his voice sounded like a child's as he searched for his mother.

"No," she chided herself. "I won't feel this way. I can do all things through Christ . . ."

"I'll see to the horses," Duffy said in a fearful voice.

Looking back on it from the vantage point of her bed that night, Hannah knew that only the Lord could have given her the strength to endure that fateful meeting with Mother Stivers. If anything else had gone wrong, Hannah would probably have collapsed. As it was, her head ached so that with each beat of her heart her temples throbbed.

When Hannah entered her home that evening, she barely recognized it. There were trunks and boxes and valises sitting all over the sitting room floor. Amidst all the disarray sat a tiny little lady on the end of one of the packing crates. Her back was ramrod straight; not a single hair escaped the severe bun on the back of her head. Hannah remembered having the irreverent thought, "I wonder if a smile has ever crossed those lips." Though it had taken Hannah and the children only a few moments to clamber down from the buggy and run into the house, evidently Will's reunion with his mother had already been accomplished. The mother did not show any emotional signs at all; not joy, not sorrow, not weariness. Will stood behind her with the strain of trying not to look disappointed very evident on his face. He addressed Hannah in a cold, almost formal tone that she had never heard before.

"Hannah, dear, this is my mother." Hannah wondered at the tone of his voice. Was it shame or fear of rejection which she thought she heard as he added hastily, "And Mother, this is my wife, Hannah."

Hannah tried to curtsy as she would have in ages past back in Germany. But she was carrying little Willy, and doing so threw her off balance. She nearly dropped the baby right in her mother-in-law's lap. The only thing that saved her from a fall was that she reached

74

out and steadied herself, grabbing the formidable little lady's arm in the process.

"Aach! No gloves . . . and her hands are as rough as burlap. See here, she has snagged my dress!" Mrs. Stivers huffed. She turned her eyes back to her son, speaking as if Hannah were not even there. The voice had a nasal whine to it, and was extremely loud.

Hannah smiled and began to apologize. "I'm sorry, Mrs. Stivers. But please, let me welcome you to our . . ." It was a speech which was never to be finished, for just then Willy set up a mighty wail. Evidently the jostling and the loud new voice frightened the babe.

Will valiantly tried to intervene. "Mother, it seems your newest grandson wants to make his presence known. This is Willy!" he exclaimed with pride, taking the baby from Hannah and holding him out to his mother.

The woman crossed her arms tightly and sniffed loudly. "I see," she mumbled. Looking past the baby and his disappointed father at Libby she said, "And who is this red-eyed little thing? You look as if you'd just lost your best friend instead of gaining a grandmother." Turning to Hannah again she demanded, "Does the child speak?"

Hannah placed her arm across Libby's shoulders and said, "Mrs. Stivers, this is Libby. She's had a trying evening of bitter disappointment."

Libby stared at the floor and mumbled, "Good evening, grandmother."

"What's that? Speak up, child!" the woman flared. "I never could tolerate people talking under their breath. What's her name?" She again addressed the question to Will as if he were the only human being present in the room. She went on, "Libby surely can't be her given name. What's it short for? Elizabeth?"

"No, Mother," Will responded, passing Willy back to Hannah. "Our daughter's name is Liberty Lucille

75

Stivers." Hannah noticed that he spoke very slowly, distinctly and louder than normal. Slowly it dawned on Hannah that Mother Stivers had a hearing problem.

"Liberty Lucille! What kind of queer name is that? And why is she blubbering around so much?"

Hannah had listened to all she could take. "Excuse me, Will ... Mrs. Stivers ... I'm going to get Willy's milk ready and put the children to bed." She walked past the two of them into the kitchen, with Libby following her.

At the doorway, Hannah glanced back to see a frantic looking Will gazing at her. "Hurry, my lady," he pleaded.

Once upstairs, Hannah laid the baby who was now dry, warm, and full of his beloved goat's milk on Libby's bed. Turning to her daughter, she pulled her long tresses out from under her flannel gown and began to brush them gently.

"Mama, she isn't at all what I expected!" the child whispered. Hannah was grateful that Libby's mind wasn't on Little Marc any more. "How shall we ever learn to get along with such a ... such a ... hateful ... old ..." Before Libby could finish the sentence, Hannah put her hand over her mouth.

"Shh," she whispered. "No matter how she seems to us now, she is your father's mother. And we shall just learn to live with her. Remember she must be extremely tired after the long sea voyage she's endured. And ... and, oh my! We've left Mrs. Stivers sitting on a packing crate!" The sudden recollection startled Hannah to action as a hostess.

"Libby, I must get back. I love you, my dear. Remember that tomorrow is another day. Say your prayers," she reminded as she picked up the baby and headed back down the stairs to the kitchen.

Libby knelt by her bed for much longer than usual that evening, trying in her own childish way to lay all

76

her burdens at her Saviour's feet.

Downstairs, Hannah put Willy in the cradle in her and Will's room and then set about making tea. When it was finished, she went to the kitchen door.

"Will, whyn't you and your mother join me out here for a warm cup of tea?"

Will glanced at her gratefully. "Ah, yes, that sounds delicious, doesn't it, Mother?" Taking her arm, he escorted his mother, talking nervously all the way. "Hannah, Mother has been getting acquainted with Duffy."

Hannah realized that she'd been so preoccupied with her own and Libby's problems that she'd never even considered her firstborn's reaction to his new grandmother.

"Come have some tea with us, Duffy," she added as an afterthought. "You deserve it for rubbing down the team and doing your Pa's share of the barn chorin' when we got home."

"Thank you anyway, Mama, but I don't think I want any tea. I'm sort of tired. I think I'll just go on up to bed if it's all right."

Hannah stared hard at her son. He was being polite as always. But there was definitely something amiss. She did not need to wonder long.

"Do none of them speak so's to be understood, son?" the grandmother asked. "Why, you and your dear brother were ne'er allowed to mumble under your breath so!" She barely took a breath before she continued. "Are you expecting me to eat in a kitchen like a common slave? And where on earth did you get such outlandish names for your children? Freedom! No wonder he goes by Duffy!"

"Goodnight, son," Hannah whispered a she patted Duffy's arm. "Don't forget to say your prayers."

"Don't worry. I shall certainly pray this night!" A knowing look passed between Hannah and Duffy.

With a quick "Goodnight," he rushed up the stairs.

And now at last all was quiet. Will's even breathing beside her told her he was fast falling asleep. But Hannah was troubled.

"Will, where shall we ever put all the things she brought? She wasn't at all happy to be herded up the stairs and to bed. I think she wanted to unpack it all tonight," Hannah whispered.

"Why are you whispering? She can't hear you in the same room," Will responded groggily.

"Why didn't you warn us of her deafness?"

"I guess I forgot. It's gotten lots worse though." He pulled Hannah into his arms. "Try not to worry, dear. It was rough going tonight, I know. But tomorrow's another day."

Hannah had to smile. Her exact words to Libby. She hoped they gave Libby more comfort than they did her. Hannah's mind spun with all sorts of problems— especially how she could ever learn to deal with this stranger who would forevermore be a part of their lives. Forever! Oh, it seemed so long and so hard. A tear escaped and slid down onto Will's chest before she could stop it. His even breathing told her he never felt it.

"I can do all things through Christ," she began. Hannah fell asleep repeating her favorite verse.

Chapter 12

uring the next several weeks, Hannah felt as if she was being torn in half by the dissension in their once-peaceful home. The children and Will's mother were constantly at odds. She often complained to Will, "I feel as if I'm playing mediator between two warring factions who have nothing in common excepting the name Stivers."

Of a truth, Will was hard put to find an answer to the dilemma. He tried to explain to Duffy and Libby that they must learn to speak loudly, slowly and distinctly when addressing Grandmother Stivers. And in turn he tried to gently convince his mother that she needed to try to fit into their lifestyle, no longer expecting to be waited on hand and foot.

" 'Tis strange how the Lord oft brings folks together through a crisis of some type, isn't it, Mother?' Hannah asked as the two ladies sat on opposite sides of the kitchen table snapping green beans. It had now been two months since Will's mother arrived.

"Aye," responded Mrs. Stivers. "I'm guessing that you are remembering the night Libby took so sick."

Hannah nodded, as once again she marvelled over

that awful night a fortnight ago.

The evening had been hot with controversy as so many had been since Mrs. Stivers arrived. The dinner had not been to her liking, so she had refused to eat a bite. Sulking in the sitting room, now crowded by her things, after the meal she had interrupted and corrected a lesson in wicking Hannah was giving to Libby.

"No, Libby, you're making French knots," Hannah said. "You want this spread to last a long time, don't you? The new knot that Aunt 'Cille learned in town from the seamstress is said to hold up in hundreds more washings than the old style French knot. Now, watch me again. You bring your wick across the needle like this in the figure of a number seven and then . . ."

"Mayhap if the child had some decent cloth to work on," the grandmother began. "And whyn't you buy her some real thread or yarn?" she added. "It seems almost heathenish to use the common wick of a candle to decorate a bedspread."

All was quiet for a moment. It was as if the entire Stivers household had reached a breaking point and collectively they sighed in despair. But 'twas Libby whose pot boiled over.

"Grandmother, *please!*" she implored. " 'Tis hard enough for me to learn to do all these womanly things without you all the time inferring that my Mama doesn't teach me properly."

Duffy gasped that Libby would so blatantly cross the bounds of what was considered speaking properly to an adult . . . let alone to the awful dowager who had so thoroughly dominated their home for six weeks. Hannah began to reprimand Libby, but Will whispered loudly, "Let her speak, my lady. 'Tis time . . . no, 'tis much *past* time."

The girl continued, trying valiantly to keep emotion out of her voice. Clearly, in a loud voice she went on. "The reason we are working the knots on this homespun material is because the price of everything is getting so dear. And that's why we Colonial ladies have begun to use the extra candlewicking to work the designs also. The king's tariffs are making the prices of yarns and threads exhorbitant. Besides, Aunt 'Cille says a candlewicked spread on homespun is just as nice as the chenille ones from the motherlands. And if I can learn to do the new knot, it will hold up much longer in the end." The child-woman had expended all her energy with the speech, and she trembled now in the aftermath.

"Well, I never!" her adversary exploded. "William, how can you allow such impudent behavior in your home against your mother? After I left my homeland and everything just to come to you and now. . . ."

But evidently Will had finally had enough.

"Mother," he interrupted, "listen to me. Libby only said what I should have said much afore this time. E'er since you arrived, you've been so defensive. You've treated Hannah and the children horribly. You expect us to wait on you as if you were a queen. But, Mother, this is America. We left the royalty and the landed gentry behind us in Europe. Here, everyone is equal and everyone pitches in and does their share of the work. Mother, we desperately wanted you to come here—all of us did! But it just isn't working out like we hoped."

The elder Mrs. Stivers stared at her son in horror. But Hannah thought she saw a glimmer of respect in her eyes replacing the contempt she had seen there before.

At that moment Duffy joined in the performance. "Grandmother, Libby and I could hardly wait for you to arrive. We never had grandparents like so many of the children at school. Libby let Papa put a wall through her bedroom to build your room. Not because she had to—because she wanted to have a grandmother she could talk to and share secrets with. But all you do is tell Papa we don't speak right and make fun of our lovely names and ..." The ever-close tears confounded Duffy again, and he ran from the room. At the door he turned and shouted, "Why won't you let us love you?" Then he raced up the stairs.

Mrs. Stivers rose from her chair, trying to muster all the dignity she could. "William, I shall retire to my room now."

Hannah thought she seemed to have aged ten years in ten minutes' time. Her perfect posture was replaced by a discouraged stoop and her loud voice was barely a whisper. "I didn't know I was such a problem. If you will drive me to town on the morrow, I shall arrange passage." Hannah couldn't bear to see Will's lovely dream end in such a shambles.

"No, Mother Stivers, please!" she interrupted. "Don't even think of leaving us."

Her mother-in-law squared her shoulders, staring into Hannah's eyes. Could it be longing Hannah saw?

"The chidren were telling the truth. We wanted you to come. I know that in your eyes I shall never be good enough for your William. I suppose I shall always be the poor servant girl who lived on the edge of your estate. But Ma'am—you see, we are not on opposite sides of that question. I know I do not deserve one so fine as your son. I have ne'er been able to understand why he chose to love me. But we believe God brought us together. Yes, the same God you taught your little boy to love all those years ago. I love that God, too. So the Bible teaches that you are my sister in Jesus. If not for your son's sake, or your grandchildren's, can't you accept me for Jesus' sake?"

Now Mrs. Stivers appeared broken. Still something kept her from reaching out to the sets of waiting arms all around her.

"I'm suddenly very tired," she mumbled. "I don't

believe I can ever get used to any of this ... this ... land! I'll never understand why ..." But the family never heard the rest of her confession for she fled the room in sobs.

"Oh, Papa, I'm so sorry," a tearful Libby cried into his shoulder. "I shouldn't have spoken."

"There, there," Will soothed. "It's best to get these things out. Don't fret, my sweet. Go back to your candlewicking. 'Twill be a lovely spread."

And so Hannah and Libby settled down by the coal oil lamp with a sigh and a shake of the head.

Later on Libby put her needle down. "I don't feel quite right, Mama. It's hard for me to breathe. Isn't it awfully warm in here?"

Hannah immediately jumped to her side. "Will, she's very hot. What shall we do?" The worried mother spoke as she felt Libby's fevered brow.

"Now, my lady, please be calm. Libby's been sneezing and coughing for a couple days. She'll be better in the morning. Let's just get her up to bed. Mayhap a hot cup of camomile tea?"

But Libby did not improve in the night. She tossed fitfully on her bed and coughed almost incessantly. About three o'clock in the morning, she called in a hoarse voice.

"Help! Help! Somebody! I can't breathe!"

Duffy rushed into his sister's room and the croaking rattle in her chest made his feet fly down the stairs.

"Mama! Papa! Come quick! It's Libby!"

Hannah raced up the stairs and caught her daughter in her arms. "Libby, baby! I was only going to lie down on the daybed in the kitchen whilst I brewed you more tea. I fell asleep. Darling, try to take deep breaths." Guilt and fear were strangling Hannah as surely as the illness in Libby's throat was choking her.

"Mama! Papa! I ... I ... it hurts! I can't get my breath!" Each word was choked out on a short gasp, with strangling coughs and croaks between.

"I'll go for Doc Hatfield," Will shouted as he raced toward the stairs tucking in his shirt as he ran.

Duffy brought a lamp into Libby's room just as his grandmother appeared in the doorway.

"How's a body to sleep? What's all the . . ." But then she looked at Libby. "Jesus, help us," she cried. "Duffy, go put lots of pots of water on the stove. Build the fire up hot. Hannah, get some sheets . . . or blankets. Be quick, dear. It's croup. We haven't much time."

Hannah raced down to her room where the extra sheets were kept folded neatly in the clothes press. No one had time to marvel at the change in the woman now clearly in charge.

"Here, Duffy. Tug the daybed over just next to the stove." Mrs. Stivers had summoned strength no one knew she possessed to carry the frightened Libby downstairs. When Hannah reentered the kitchen, she was just placing Libby on her side on the daybed. "Lie still, my pet. Grandmama is here. We'll make it so you can breathe."

Libby was crying and gasping for breath. To Hannah it seemed horribly cruel to place her so near the hot fire and all the water pots beginning to boil.

"Hannah, the sheets!" Mrs. Stivers ordered. "Help me make a tent over Libby! And over the stove!"

"Ma . . . gasp . . . ma! Cough . . . please! I . . . can't . . . I'm scared!"

"No! She'll suffocate!" Hannah tried to pull the sheet away from Libby's face. "You're scaring her!"

Mrs. Stivers took hold of Hannah's arm, gently but firmly. "Hannah, trust me, like you seemed to want earlier for me to trust you. It's croup! William had it as a child. She has to breathe the steam, else she *will* suffocate!"

In one brief moment of time the two women joined forces to save Libby's life. Hannah helped erect a tent of sheets over Libby and the stove covered with pots of boiling water. Mrs. Stivers, Duffy, and Hannah held the sheets and each prayed silently. Libby's sobs grew desperate from fear at first, but soon she began to cough less, breathe easier, and the choking stopped.

She had just mumbled, "It doesn't hurt," when Will and Doc Hatfield burst in the back door.

"Where's Libby?" the frightened father shouted.

"I'm here, Papa . . . in a tent!" came the feeble reply.

"Your mother definitely saved Libby's life with this steam tent idea," Doc Hatfield said as the four adults sat at the table at dawn. The doctor had mixed some powders which he said would let Libby sleep several hours. "Wherever did you learn how to deal with the croup, Ma'am?"

Mrs. Stivers took a long drink of tea before responding. "When William was a toddler, we almost lost him many times to attacks such as Libby just suffered. I'd forgotten how horrible it is. My heart just ached for you, Hannah. I was so afraid it was too late. But, to answer your question, Doctor, 'twas one of our servant girls on the estate who told us to use steam all those years ago."

"A wise lassie she must have been. From all ye've told me, it turned the tide for Miss Liberty tonight."

In the two weeks hence, the family had become a solid unit of love and loyalty, much as Will had envisioned when he first wrote to his mother inviting her to America.

The beans were nearly ready to start cooking now. Mother Stivers smiled shyly at Hannah.

"I don't know how I shall e'er make up for my actions that first six weeks here in your home. I was just so full of bitterness over losing my husband and Will's older brother and the castle that I just could not allow myself to be hurt again. I kept telling myself that none of you *really* wanted me here. And I didn't want

85

to love any of you because I couldn't face how it would hurt if I were to lose you, too. But that awful night when we almost lost Libby, well—I realized I already did love her and all of you. I'm like Naomi in the Bible. I used to be bitter from all I'd lost. Now ... dear Hannah ... I'm thankful for all I've gained."

" 'Tis we who have gained, Mother," Hannah said as they embraced over the beans. She smiled as she realized that Will's mother now truly felt like her mother as well.

"But Hannah, there's something that has oft bothered me. If 'tis true that you all really wanted me here, why did Libby cry so much that first night I came?"

"Aah—now Mother, *that's* a long story! And one which just reminds me of how desperately we need your advice in helping to raise these children of ours. You see ..."

Chapter 13

hen Libby was an adult she would oft look back on that summer as the most growing time in her life. It was a summer of much change. Some of the changes were welcome. Others were not.

It all began with the end-of-school assembly and picnic on the last day of May. Each child had a piece to recite. Duffy and Libby drilled each other until they could say theirs backwards as well as forwards. 'Twouldn't do to embarrass their new grandmother by forgetting one's lines.

The day dawned bright and clear. A pre-dawn shower had washed the earth and cooled things down just enough to make the day a delight. The children were dressed and ready to go quite early. The women were busy packing sumptuous fare for the picnic. Will had gone out to get the wagon ready and hitch the horses.

Suddenly an excited Duffy burst into the kitchen. "Mama, Grandmama . . ." he whispered. "Come into the front room . . . but come quietly. It's a surprise!" Suddenly realizing his grandmother couldn't hear him, he gestured elaborately, beckoning with his right hand while his left hand made a "Shh" sign at his lips.

The ladies could tell by Duffy's ear-to-ear grin that something wondrous was happening. As the door to the kitchen swung open and they saw the scene before them, gasps escaped every mouth.

There in the middle of the sitting room floor stood a tottery baby Willy. His back was to his Mama as she entered the room. Libby sat on the edge of a chair opposite the door. Keeping her voice calm and without looking at anyone but the baby, she said, "Can you believe it? He crawled over to the sofa and pulled himself up. Then he turned around and started to walk as if he'd done it a thousand times before. So far, he's taken ten steps!"

Mother Stivers started to rush into the room, but knowing that getting startled would make him fall, Hannah restrained her. Hannah's eyes were filling with tears as she said, "Bless the Lord. There were so many times I thought we'd not raise this one. 'Tis a miracle for sure that he's strong enough to walk ... and just barely nine months old!"

"Come on, Willy. Come to your sister," Libby coaxed. She dropped down to her knees on the floor and extended her arms before her.

The baby flapped his arms excitedly and giggled. The action nearly threw him off balance. He regained his control and took six more steps nearly at a run, directly into his sister's arms.

The older people in the room all began babbling at once.

"Such a big fine boy!"

"Why, him's just a little man, isn't him?"

"A genius, that's what! Whoever heard of a baby walking at nine months!"

Entering the house to hurry his family, Will heard what sounded like a henhouse chorus. Then he learned that William Justice was walking. Taking the babe in his arms, he joined momentarily in the hubbub. But then he announced, "Walking baby brother or not, Duff and Lib must get to the schoolhouse soon."

Hannah carried a picnic basket while Mrs. Stivers brought a pie in each hand. All bounded into the wagon and they were off.

The school program went off without any problems, except in the eyes of Mr. Sluss, the pedagogue, who was never satisfied, even with perfection. As always, the smallest children recited first. Libby was quoting her poem through in her mind, and didn't realize her turn had come until Mr. Sluss hissed, "Liberty Stivers, *if you please!*"

The red-faced woman-child took her place on the raised platform beside the teacher's desk and began. "The quality of mercy is not strained." Mr. Shakespeare's work was not easy to recite but she made it through the stanza in short order. Then with a mischievous grin she added without missing a beat, "And by the way, baby Willy can walk!" With a deep curtsy, amid laughter and applause, she left the platform and returned to her seat. Duffy winked at his sister, while Mr. Sluss glared over his pince-nez.

The last student to recite that day was Little Marc Woodcutter. He had memorized a long passage of Scripture from the book of Isaiah. It ended with a picture in words which had long been a favorite verse of many of the audience. Years ago someone in their parish had set them to music. Unbeknown to the prim and proper Mr. Sluss, when Marc came to the beloved verse, he began to sing, motioning everyone to join him. And so it was that the program concluded with an almost church-like atmosphere. A passerby could hear beautiful four-part harmony singing a cappella: "They that wait upon the Lord shall renew their strength, they shall mount up with wings as eagles. They shall run and not be weary. They shall walk and not faint."

After the last notes had died away, awards were given for best scholar (Little Marc, naturally), best penmanship, and perfect attendance. The party moved out of doors and collectively, the community breathed a sigh of relief—another school year was past.

All the girls in the school had planned a box social for the noon hour. The effervescent Mrs. Karla Witherspoon had volunteered to act as auctioneer. Each girl had packed every special delicacy she could make, or coax her mother into making, into a box lunch. Just enough for two people. The boxes were then gaily decorated and now all stood in a row awaiting bidding. The boys of the community placed bids, the money being given to the church's newly organized Sunday School. For every girl it was an anxious time, wondering who she would get to, or be forced to, dine with.

Mrs. Witherspoon was now holding up a beautiful box. It was not gaudy. In fact, it was very simply done, but so elegant. The paper was white, tied with a ribbon of red gingham checked material. Inserted artfully into the bow was one perfect red rose. "And what am I bid on this lovely box?" Sniffing appreciatively Karla added, "Oh, boys! I believe I smell southern fried chicken." The bidding began at one cent but Little Marc kept raising the price. Several boys seemed interested in this box. A sad Libby realized Little Marc would not stop bidding until he owned the box. All her efforts on her own box would come to naught.

"He doesn't even like chicken," she mumbled.

But just then Karla giggled. "Going—going—gone! Well, Little Marc, for the hefty price of seventy-eight cents, it seems you've purchased the right to dine with" ... All was hushed as she opened the sealing wax ... "Ah—Miss Emily Gibson!"

"I will not cry. I will not cry," Libby whispered to herself. But, oh, how her heart ached. Grandmother Stivers and Hannah exchanged sad knowing glances and silent prayers were sent heavenward on behalf of their Libby.

Duffy had chosen to bid on the box of his long-time playmate, Hannah Witherspoon. A gangly pimple-faced boy named Tom bought Libby's box. Except for Emily and Little Marc, the children all just sat together on blankets in the schoolyard eating and joking. Soon there were games of jumping rope and stick-ball and jackstones going everywhere.

Libby came to Hannah when she heard Willy crying and said, "I will give him his bottle, Mama whilst you visit with the ladies." At first Hannah protested that she should run on and play, but something in Libby's haunted eyes stopped her.

"All right, dear," she said as she handed over the sleepy toddler. "Mayhap you could take him to the wagon. We'll be leaving soon, if you're agreein'?"

"Oh, yes, I'm more than ready," mumbled Libby.

As she sat on the back of the buckboard cuddling her heavy baby brother, a movement at the edge of the woods caught her eye. Though she turned her back quickly, she would never forget the scene she saw as Little Marc and Emily Gibson stole a secret kiss. No one but baby Willy saw the tears as they fell. Thankfully, he was too young to understand. But his fat little fist entangled in her hair was a comfort to the heartbroken girl.

From inside the schoolhouse Karla Witherspoon turned from the window. "I tell you, Hannah, you should let Libby put her hair up. I care not what her age is. She is the most mature of all the girls here. Why, just look at her out there loving baby Willy. She'll make a wonderful mother and wife to someone, and before e'er long I'm predicting."

* * * * * * * * * * *

With freedom from the classroom came the work of the farm. Libby helped in the garden daily while Will and Duffy worried over the crops.

"I'm telling ya, my lady, the fields are tired. They've been planted and worked till they've nothin' left to give," Will complained almost nightly. "That's why in Germany my father would allow a field to lie fallow for two years. To let it rest. But, we're so hemmed in with people everywhere that we can't let any field rest. For there are no new fields to plant. We must keep reusing them just to break even. And it seems break even is all we're ever going to do."

Hannah listened patiently to her husband's grumbles. She knew he was right. It was hard to even remember how things used to be. Why, when she and Will arrived here in America, the Woodcutters' mansion had been surrounded by forests. Their own humbler abode had been even farther away from the city. But now ... why, the road out front had recently received a new load of fresh stone and gravel. What had once been a tiny path was becoming the main route west out of Norfolk. As the road grew, it seemed to pull houses, stores, and buildings in its wake.

Glancing out the window Hannah could see rooftops of her neighbors and could even smell the fire Mrs. Cudahy across the road had used all day to make a summer's supply of lye soap. "Oh, Will," she stammered, "I wish we could go back. I know you were so much happier when we weren't so closed in by folks. If only we'd a thought ahead and bought up the properties when Marc decided to sell them when the lumber had all been cut off of them. But who would ever have thought the city would grow so?"

Will interrupted. "Laying aside our financial need and the need for breathing room for a moment, why— I hardly consider Virginia to be a free country any more. What with England a makin' folks pay money for stamps. To get married you need a stamp. To get buried you need a stamp. It's ridiculous. Soon there'll be a law that to breathe you need a stamp!"

"Mayhap if England was our motherland 'stead of Germany you'd feel more loyalty to her," the tired wife responded.

"I think not!" Will argued passionately. "Why, my lady, if it were Germany tellin' people they had to provide quarters for soldiers, I'd be just as upset as I am about Grenville's Quartering Act of 1765! I'm tellin' you, Hannah, if they ever try to put a redcoat in my house . . ."

"Will, please stop! You know how I hate all the talk of rebellion and revolt you hear everywhere!" There were tears at the edge of her voice. "I hate seeing you so unhappy. I wish I could make you happy."

"Aach, my lady, stop!" Will whispered. Whenever he was emotional the old German phrasing slipped into his speech unawares. "I am happy, Hannah. You make me happy. And the children. Why, I'm greatly blessed by God. I've no right to complain. Forgive me, please?"

And so once again they avoided discussing what was now an obsession with Will—the desire to move.

Summer's heat descended like a cloud. Though Libby and Hannah carried pail after pail of water to their thirsty truck patch, the vegetables shrivelled on the vines. A great malaise seemed to grip the family, nay—the community. The talk everywhere, when not political, was of the need for rain. No one could remember a summer to equal this. One could not even rock in a rocking chair without working up a sweat. Everyone constantly looked at the sky hoping to see clouds. But, its relentless blue returned all their stares.

Chapter 14

I t was nearing harvest time, but there would certainly be no need of the big threshing parties this year. No one was sure if there would be anything to harvest at all. The drought had nearly ruined the tired farms of the area.

But business continued at a flurry for the Norfolk Lumber Company. All the new buildings everywhere gave Marc Woodcutter more orders than he could fill.

It was hard for Karla and Louisa to get Marc to take even one day off for a party. But the two girls were determined that Little Marc would not leave for college without a proper send-off. In the middle of August all the Stivers, Woodcutters, and Witherspoon families gathered at Louisa's home for a farewell. The food was delicious but hearts were heavy and laughter seemed forced.

Libby thought she had accepted the fact of Little Marc's infatuation with Emily. Deep inside she always hoped that it was nothing more than infatuation. That some day he would wake up and realize that she, Libby, was the only girl for him. So the announcement seemed like an arrow aimed straight at her heart.

After Little Marc had opened the few gifts—some fine writing paper, warm slippers, and a new horse blanket—he stood and cleared his throat. His voice was so low and he so tall that Hannah caught her breath.

"Why, Little Marc is a man fully grown!" she thought. And his announcement proved her correct.

"Folks, I want to thank you all for this fine send-off. I—uh, well . . . I don't say it . . . but I love and appreciate all of you. Papa, I know you would have loved it if I had joined you at Norfolk Lumber. But I hope you understand the burning desire I have to study law."

Mister Marc's eyes were bright as he interrupted his son. " 'Twas settled long ago, Marc. Before you chidren were born, we told God to use you how e'er He saw fit. If He wants you in law, then we do, too!"

Next Little Marc turned to his sisters. "Karla, Louisa —how can I ever thank you both for all you've done for me? This is the second lovely party you've given me."

Karla spoke. " 'Tisn't a party really. Why, we're all just family."

Louisa gave her brother a hug. "You've no reason to thank us. We enjoy doing for you. We don't often admit it, but you are a pretty good brother. And . . . and, I'm gonna miss you somethin' awful."

Her carefree husband, Daniel, interrupted. "Let your brother have his say, Louisa. And don't go blubbering all over his shoulder."Laughter all around eased the moment.

Then Little Marc turned to his adopted family, the Stivers. "Aunt Hannah, Uncle Will, . . . I don't know how to say what is in my heart. Your home has always been my other home. I believe I shall miss it almost as much as my own home." His voice broke, but he continued. "Duffy, old man, you've been like a brother to me. I'll ne'er forget all our fishing times, and everything else we've done."

Now his eyes fell on Libby, though he still spoke directly to Duffy. "I want your solemn promise, Duffy—before God and all these witnesses . . ."

Chad Witherspoon interjected, "Already he talks like a lawyer!"

When the laughter died down, he continued. "Anyway, Duffy—you promise me to take care of the little girl who grew up overnight to become Miss Liberty Lucille Stivers. She's gotten so beautiful I don't even feel like I know her any more, but she'll always be the fun little tomboy in my memories. Be happy, Libby—and I bet some day soon you will make some man happy."

How Little Marc could have been so blind to the love on Libby's face, Hannah would never know. As he proceeded around the room to give a special word to each niece and nephew, Libby dropped her eyes and wept openly. But no one thought a thing about it, for nearly everyone was crying.

At last Little Marc came to his mother. After a long pause, he said, "Mama, I love you. I always will. I know you have been awfully worried about me going so far away alone. And so, I hope you can be happy for me, instead of angry, when I tell you I shall not be going alone."

The room was hushed. Whatever did the boy mean?

"Come here, my dear," he said turning to the hallway. "Everyone, please welcome Mrs. Marcus Phillip Woodcutter. We were married this afternoon."

As he spoke, Emily Gibson walked into the doorway. She looked lovely as ever in a navy blue travelling suit with white collar and cuffs. The matching hat she wore had a short veil down to her nose. Her hands visibly shook, and there were red splotches appearing on her face. Her blond curls were tucked demurely into a twisted coiffure. Just before she dropped her eyes to the floor she whispered, "Hello everyone." Hannah noticed tears in her eyelashes.

For a moment the silence was deafening. But then the room exploded with sound as everyone jumped to hug the new bride, congratulate the groom, welcome Emily into the family, scold them for the secret wedding, and just generally celebrate.

Amidst all the hubbub, Libby sat wondering if her world would ever come right again. She felt a thin arm encircle her shoulders like a vise. "Buck up, Miss Liberty. Go congratulate them. You are a Stivers, after all." With a quick kiss on her cheek, Grandmother released her, and shoved her out of the chair. Libby looked at her grandmother in confusion, but the pride she saw gleaming in the old lady's eyes made her want to do what she knew she must.

"Congratulations, Emily," she said. And somehow, with the saying, came the feeling. When she said, "I hope you will be very happy," she meant it. Then she stumbled over to where Little Marc stood drinking a toast of cider to his wife. He turned away from his joking brothers-in-law, his father, Will, and Duffy. For just the briefest moment it was as if she and he were the only two in the room. Their eyes were locked in a soul-searching gaze.

"Please be happy for me, Lib. I mean, uh ... I know how you feel. But you must understand ... to me you were always a little sister. When you grew up so fast this year, I tried to love you back, but it just wouldn't happen for me."

He knew! Her eyes dropped in shame as a deep blush began at her neck and crept upward.

But Little Marc reached out and gently pulled her chin up, forcing her to face him. There were tears in his eyes too, as he whispered. "It'll happen for you some day Lib—just like it did for Emily and me. And when it does, you'll understand. Till then, I only hope you will ... will try to ..."

She couldn't let him stumble on in agony any longer.

She reached up and gave him a kiss on the cheek. "Oh, Marc, do be happy. I really want that. I'll miss you."

And in so saying, a little part of Libby Stivers died. Hopes that she had carried for over half of her life fizzled before her eyes. No one could ever have convinced her that one day there would be a resurrection of that part of herself for she felt it was buried forever.

The newlyweds delayed their departure for Williamsburg for one day. One day in which so many gifts were bestowed on them that instead of riding Little Marc's horse double as he had planned it, they drove off in a buggy to their new life at William and Mary College. A friend in Norfolk had arranged for them to live in his mother's house in Williamsburg. Emily could tend to the elderly lady's needs while Marcus received his education. Of course, with the Woodcutter fortunes to back them, there were no financial clouds on the couple's horizon.

And once again life settled into a routine of watching the weather for the Stivers family.

* * * * * * * * * * *

The onset of fall brought no relief from the heat and drought. The fields were harvested, but the silo was only half filled with corn for the animals to eat. And even that corn was only nubbins when compared to yields of the earlier years.

Will developed a haunted look in his eyes that began to plague Hannah. One day as she and Lucille were putting a quilt in the frame together, she began to cry softly.

"Hush, Hannah dear. I know 'tis a tedious task and it always is hard to stretch the quilt as tight as it needs to be, but we'll get it in. We always do!"

"Oh, Mistress," Hannah shook her head as she sobbed, not even realizing she'd slipped into the name she'd used sixteen years earlier when she worked for the Woodcutters. " 'Tisn't the quilt that troubles me. It's Will."

Their task forgotten for the time being, the two ladies went to the kitchen for tea. At Lucille's house, the big maid Samantha would have served tea. But Hannah had no servants nor would she have wanted them if the Stivers had been equal in wealth to the Woodcutters. As she poured the hot liquid into the cups, she poured forth her heart as well.

"Will is so unhappy here. It's been coming on for years. But I've tried to ignore it. I thought when his mother arrived that would surely make him more content. But it has only heightened his longing to move westward. Last evening we had a discussion about it."

Lucille asked, "And what did he say in this . . . uh . . . discussion?"

Hannah nodded, coloring slightly. "As always, you can read my mind. 'Twas more like an argument. He just asked me again if I couldn't try to consider the advantages in moving to the west. He almost begged me, really."

"Well, and what turned his request into an argument then, dear?"

"Oh, Lucille, I don't know what's wrong with me really. In my heart, I know he is right. Moving is the only sensible thing for us to do. There's not much future for us here with the land so overworked. If we stay here, I just know Will and Duffy will get involved with that secret group, the Sons of Liberty, and I am so frightened. But, it has been so good for me to have a home all these years. I just hate to give it all up."

"Exacty what do you hate to leave?"

"Why, everything! The house, the feeling of safety, friends . . . the three little crosses on the hill."

"Oh, Hannah. I know it must hurt to think of leaving those little darlings behind. But we both know they aren't really there anyway. Those three babes and my little Marta have been playing on the golden streets of heaven for all these years."

Of course Hannah knew Lucille was right. Sometimes she forgot about the darling little girl they'd buried at sea all those years ago.

Her friend interrupted her thoughts. "You know, I don't believe those who have gone on ahead of us would want us to let their memories keep us stymied from moving forward in our lives. You must think about your living children."

"Yes, I know," Hannah muttered as she poured them each more tea. "And when I do that, I know we should move. Duffy wants to go so badly."

"He never has enjoyed school, has he?"

"No, he's begging Will not to make him return this year. Last evening he said, 'School was fine for Little Marc. He's wanted to be a lawyer since we were little. After he learns all he can at William and Mary, he'll study with a lawyer up there in Williamsburg. But Papa, I hate it. I know all I need to know to farm. And as soon as I'm old enough, I'm moving to Ohio. I've got all the education I need to live on the frontier.' He is so much bigger than the other students. I think if I were him, I shouldn't want to return either."

"What about Libby? Does she wish to move?"

Hannah had never disclosed Libby's heartbreak to her friend, not wishing to worry her when there was no help for Libby other than time's healing. "Oh, it's so hard to tell what Libby wants. She just sort of mopes around, doing whatever she is told, but with none of her old enthusiasm for life. Mayhap it would be a welcome change for her if we would move."

Lucille interjected a thought of her own. "Well, at least Willy is young enough that you needn't fret about what he wants."

"Yes," smiled Hannah. "And now that he is finally able to drink cow's milk, we wouldn't have the worry of the goats."

"What about Will's mother?" her friend whispered.

"Oh, you needn't lower your voice. She's napping upstairs, but even if she wasn't, she couldn't hear you. Believe it or not, I think Mrs. Stivers could be happy anywhere as long as we were all together. Once she cut her ties to the castle, it's as if she decided never to make any emotional ties to any thing again. She dotes on the children and Will to a fault. But I really can't complain, for she seems to love me too. I tried to feel her out about the idea of moving the other day. She said, 'Oh, wouldn't that be a grand adventure?' But when she saw me frowning she quickly added, 'But whatever you and William decide is fine with me. I shall be happy wherever we are all together.' "

A long pause ensued. Lucille asked quietly, "And what of you Hannah? Can you be happy if you are all together?"

The tears began afresh. She took her friend's hand. "I'm so afraid. Surely you have heard the horrible stories of the Indians. What if ..." She couldn't even put words to her fears.

"Hannah dear. Don't let fear of the unknown keep you from fulfilling your family's destiny. Don't you remember what the Bible says in the book of Hebrews? I think it is in chapter thirteen. 'For He hath said, I will never leave thee, nor forsake thee. So that we may boldly say, The Lord is my helper, and I will not fear what man shall do unto me.' "

Hannah sat still and let the words penetrate her aching heart. Softly she repeated, "I will not fear what man shall do unto me. Indians are men, after all, aren't they?" Slowly a smile emerged. "Oh, Lucille," she exclaimed, "why didn't I talk to you about this a long time ago? You always help me to see things more clearly. But, oh, dear—if we move, I shall still miss you and Marc and the girls so desperately."

Now it was Lucille's turn to fight tears. "Oh, Hannah, I know. It seems impossible to me to face a future without your friendship close. But all of life is change. And we mustn't refuse to make the necessary changes else somehow I think we thwart God's plans for us. If it really is God leading Will to make this move, He will give us the strength to bear whatever comes." They embraced briefly, but then the ever practical Lucille said, "Now, c'mon. We have to get this quilt in the frame or I'll count today as a total waste."

* * * * * * * * * * *

That evening after supper Hannah left the dishes to the competent hands of her daughter and her mother-in-law. "Let's go for a walk, Will."

Will looked startled at her happy tone of voice. There had been so much tension between them of late. They walked silently to the little hill and each knelt to pull some weeds from the little crosses. Will helped her to her feet saying, "Oh, my lady. It seems such a long time ago at some times. And others it seems yesterday we held these babies."

Hannah brightened and took his hand in hers boldly. " 'Tis such a lovely night. Couldn't we walk down by the creek?"

" 'Tisn't much of a creek any more. This year's been so dry there's hardly a drop of water in it," he responded moodily, but turned down the side of the hill away from the house nevertheless.

"Libby seemed a bit less downhearted today. It's been three weeks since Little Marc and Emily left. Lucille said they had a letter from them in yesterday's post. Everything is fine with the newlyweds, I gather."

Hannah noticed that Will kept glancing toward the setting sun. Every so often he said, "Mmhmm" as she kept up her chatter but she knew he wasn't listening.

"Now is the time," she thought to herself and

plunged ahead as they reached the dry stream bed. "I wonder . . . when we get to Ohio, will there be awful droughts like this year?"

Will was so distracted that he mumbled, "I don't know."

"I guess there's no point in Duffy going back to school. If we'd start right away, mayhap we could be there afore the first snow. I do hope that by the time Willy is old enough there will be a real school on the frontier, but I suppose if there isn't I could . . ."

Hannah's sentence remained unfinished as Will spun her around and shouted, "What did you say?"

Smiling, Hannah answered coolly. "Which do you mean, dear? About starting right away or a school by the time Willy is old enough?"

Dumbfounded, Will's eyes filled with tears. "Hannah, my sweet lady, do you mean you're agreein' to move to Ohio?" he whispered.

"Yes, Will. I've been prayin' and cryin' and thinkin' all day on it. If you're still a mind to, I say let's do it."

He pulled her into the tightest embrace and gave her the most passionate kiss they'd shared in months. Oh, it felt so good to have the wall between them gone. "I love you, my lady," he said huskily. She leaned against him for a moment. Then he pulled away and said, "The sun is nigh down. Let's race home."

They ran like two school children until Hannah pulled up, panting, "Go on, dear. I'll catch up. I know you are dying to tell Duffy the news." Will trotted off, stopping to blow her a kiss at the springhouse.

The children were behaving as if it was Christmas. Duffy had evidently read everything in print about this wondrous land of Ohio, for he had Libby enthralled with stories. The sparkle in her daughter's eyes made Hannah know she had made the right decision. Even Willy was more vocal than usual tonight, jabbering away with Grandmama. If she was quiet as she popped

103

corn to add to the festivities, no one seemed to notice.

Will found her in the kitchen wiping a tear from her eye. "What is it Hannah? Are you already sorry?"

"No, Will. I was just thinking about the Woodcutters."

He sobered. "I know," he patted her arm. "But the children . . ." and he was off through the door to join the planners.

Just after the children were kissed goodnight and sent upstairs, there was a knock at the door. "The latch string is out. Come in," Hannah shouted as she was busy with embroidery and Will was rocking Willy.

In burst Marc and Lucille, laughing and talking and each trying to be the first to tell their news. It was total confusion.

Hannah interrupted them. "Please! Please! Sit down and talk one at a time. Whatever has you so excited?"

Lucille began. "I told Marc about our talk today. I know I tried to be brave and say all the proper things to you, but now I can tell you it left me pretty shook up, Hannah."

Will responded. "The only bad thing about our decision is leaving you folks behind."

"But that's just it!" Marc could keep their news no longer. "Ya see, Will, old man—ya aren't the only body who's been dissatisfied for a long time. Me? I'm gettin' too old to be climbin' and sawin' lumber. But I hate being stuck in the office of Norfolk Lumber Company all the time. And I don't relish all the arguments that are brewin' between old Mother England and these colonies. So when I heard you was thinkin' of movin' I said to 'Cille here, 'Whyn't we invite ourselves to go along?' We've been discussin' it all day. I'll sell the business, and we'll all head west together."

"But what about the children?" asked an incredulous Hannah.

Lucille sobered a bit. "Well, we've talked about that,

too. Little Marc and Emily will likely never settle in Norfolk anyway. Mayhap it is motherly pride, but I think my son will be leadin' this country—or at least Virginia—in some capacity some day. As for Karla and Chad and Louisa and Daniel—well, they're living their own lives. Sometimes we feel like outsiders with them. They're so busy all the time. Marcus has offered to sell the business to both of the boys but likely they will own the glass works some day, the way they're a workin' at it. Anyway, we've prayed on it and decided that iffen you'll have us, we'll join your trek to Ohio."

Hannah knew her best friend was hurting deeply over the lack of concern the girls showed their parents. But inside Hannah was so jubilant she could conceal it no longer.

The four of them met at the center of the room in a massive bear hug which woke the baby up and started him howling. Laughter and tears all mixed. After Hannah put Willy to bed, they sat at the kitchen table making plans until the wee hours of the morning.

In bed that night, Hannah spoke. "Will, when will I ever learn that God really does mean *all*?"

"What are you talking about?" her sleepy husband responded.

"You know. In Saint Matthew, chapter six, verse thirty-three. If we seek God and his kingdom first, all these things shall be added unto us. I finally let go of my fears and told God that if He was truly leading us west, I'd go. I thought I'd lost my best friends forever. But when I decided to seek God first, then He gave me *all*."

"So, you're saying Marc and Lucille are 'all these things.' Hmmm . . . wonder what they'd think about being called things?"

"Oh, Will," she gave him a playful pat. "You know what I mean."

"Goodnight Hannah," he said with a yawn.

Chapter 15

ow could such lovely plans
for the future have all run
awry? The Stivers were to
wonder this many times in
the next month or so. It had
been mid-September when Hannah had finally agreed
to move. The entire family now in agreement, each
member began to decide which of his or her things
could be sold or given away. Basically, they had come
down to nothing but clothing and the barest necessities
of household goods. For everything was to be loaded in
one large wagon. Will and Duffy worked late every
evening constructing a cover for this wagon. It would
be canvas stretched taut over a wooden framework.
Thus, should they run into any foul weather, their
belongings would be protected.

The weather was often spoken of. Could they leave
in late October and arrive in Ohio before the hard
winter set in? Most folks consulted thought they
should wait out the winter and move in the spring. But
once the hard decisions had been made, everyone
concerned was anxious to go.

Looking back, Hannah would always remember the
first feeling of foreboding she had. The Woodcutters

were at their house for a victory celebration. Less than one week after their plans to move were made known via friends and relatives, the Norfolk Lumber Company had been sold.

"Yes, sir," Marc exclaimed as he waved the money in the air. "Who e'er would have thought there'd be someone just waitin' to pay cash money for my company? I thought I'd have to make a loan available and let someone pay me on time. But it seems this 'ere Mr. Blackburn just got offen a boat from England and was just itchin' to buy himself a lumber company. That was his business back home in the motherland so he was mighty pleased to be able to buy my place. We can probably leave a mite earlier than expected now, Will."

"Mother Stivers, do you feel alright?" Lucille asked, not caring that she'd changed the subject. For the old lady had been helping Hannah mash the potatoes. Suddenly she was holding onto the stove, eyes closed, and swaying back and forth.

The grandmother coughed a wheezy, gut-wrenching cough, then answered. "Oh, yes, I'm fine. I just get a little dizzy sometimes. Mayhap I'll just sit a spell."

Hannah ran to bring her mother-in-law a cool drink from the bucket on the dry sink. "Here, Mother. You just sit . . . Libby can mash the potatoes."

The adults in the room exchanged worried glances over the old lady's head, and Hannah had an awful sense that something was wrong which would change their plans. For the rest of the evening, there were no incidents save a few spells of the horrible coughing which were becoming very frequent for Mrs. Stivers.

By the next day, however, everyone knew that Grandmother was a very sick lady indeed. The horrible coughing would go on and on until you held your breath wondering if each gasp might be her last. In the night she had begun to burn with fever. Hannah and Will stayed at her bedside that morning while Duffy drove the buckboard into town to get Doc Hatfield.

"Drop Libby and Willy off at Aunt 'Cille's on the way, Duff. I'm sending a note explaining," Hannah said in one of the brief intervals away from Will's mother. She was heating some broth on the stove. "I only pray we've gotten Libby out in time. If she were to get this with her weakness toward croup, I don't know . . ."

"What is it, Mama? Is Grandmama going to die?" the frightened young man asked.

"I don't know. I've ne'er heard a cough like this anywhere. Listen! It's got such an awful, funny sound afore she finally chokes on the cough."

Just as Doc Hatfield entered the house later that day, Mrs. Stivers was in a paroxysm of coughing. As he sprinted up the steps two at a time, there was a short silence, followed by the sound of her sucking in a breath with terrible force. He stood in the doorway of the room, taking in the entire situation at a glance. Hannah was carrying away a dishpan full of sputum. Will held a cooling damp cloth on his mother's brow and with tears in his eyes was asking, "Mother, do you know we are here?" The glazed look in the lady's eyes told the physician that she was out of her head with fever. She gasped for breath once more.

"Lord have mercy, it's the whooping cough!" Doc Hatfield exclaimed. "Where's Libby?"

Hannah nodded, knowing the doctor's concern for his croup-prone patient. "I've sent her and Willy to the Woodcutters."

"I hope you got them out of here in time. As for her, I'll have to bleed her," he explained as he took the jar of horrible looking leeches out of his black case.

The next several days were like a nightmare to the Stivers. Will and Hannah took turns, one sleeping in Libby's room just beyond the wall, while the other stayed with the aged mother. Duffy slept on the daybed in the kitchen, cared for the livestock, tried to put together meals for his parents and himself, but mostly stayed outdoors. The doctor came every day. Sometimes he bled Mother Stivers. Other times he mixed powders in hot water and tried to spoon the liquid into her mouth. But from the beginning the situation seemed hopeless. He tried to prepare them.

"Will, Hannah . . . she's resting quietly . . . come out in the hall a moment."

They followed the doctor. Mrs. Stivers hadn't moved at all in two days. Only the labored breathing and the coughing spells showed that she was still alive.

"I've done all I can do. She's in the hands of Almighty God now," the doctor explained.

"Will she . . ." Will shook his head as tears broke loose and coursed down his cheeks.

Doc Hatfield put his arm around Will. "I don't know. The next twenty-four hours will tell. But it doesn't look good."

"Can she hear us, Doctor?" Hannah asked.

"Doubtful. But it never hurts to try to talk to 'em."

Will went back and knelt at his mother's side. "I love you, Mama!" he exclaimed through his tears.

Hannah turned to go to him, but the wise doctor restrained her. "Let him be, Hannah. He needs to talk it out with her. As for you, listen to me. I've checked on Libby and Willy every day. It appears you got them out of here in time."

"Praise be," Hannah mumbled.

"Yes, but listen. I think the old lady will die tonight. If so, I want you to burn all the bedding in this room. Throw away the washpans, everything you've used. And don't let Libby come home until the funeralizing is all past and you've totally cleaned and aired this room."

Hannah looked disgusted and confused. But the doctor continued. "Please, Hannah. I know my esteemed colleagues don't agree with me. Most say 'tis only the will of God that determines whether someone gets an illness or not. And I'll grant you that I can't prove my beliefs. But I think there's something that causes diseases like this, though I know not what to call it. I just don't want Libby and Willy to come into a house that still has whatever that is in it. Do you understand?"

"Yes, doctor. We'll do as you ask."

As predicted, Mrs. Stivers did pass away that night. Hannah sat at her bedside, dozing a bit herself. Will was asleep in Libby's bed. Suddenly Hannah realized the labored breathing had stopped. She turned up the wick on the lamp and saw that a look of sweet peace was on her mother-in-law's face.

"Will, darling." She shook her exhausted husband awake. "It's over. She's gone."

Will was extremely quiet. "I hope ... I hope she knew ... that I loved her," he choked as silent tears ran freely.

"She did, darling. I'm sure of it. Why, just the day or so afore she took sick she told me she ne'er dreamed such happiness could be hers as she found here with us."

He was up now and getting dressed for all the tasks still ahead of them. Briefly they embraced. Hannah spoke softly. "I shall always be glad that she spent the last half year of her life with us. I loved her too, Will." They cried together.

* * * * * * * * * * *

The funeralizing as Doc Hatfield called it was much quicker than usual. Unbeknown to his parents, Duffy had already built his grandmother's coffin and within a few days everything was back to normal ... or to a new kind of normal. Libby had grieved and been petulant for a few days over not being allowed to attend the brief service and the meal. But now even that was in the past. The children were home and all were once again making plans for the upcoming move.

"She wouldn't have wanted to change our plans. I'm certain of that," Will said. Hannah wondered if he was trying to convince himself.

"Ya certainly needn't feel guilty 'bout going, Will," Marc interjected. "I'm sure your mother would want it." And so the talk once again turned to how many barrels of flour, corn, seed potatoes, etc. should be taken. They had decided that Duffy would drive a small buckboard full of supplies behind the two huge family wagons.

One morning Hannah awoke early. The evening before had been unseasonably warm for November so the bedroom window was open. The sky to the east was still dark, but to the north there was a curious red glow. Then she knew what had awakened her. Smoke! Running to the window she shouted, "Will! Fire! And, Dear God, help us, I'm almost sure it's Marc's woods!"

Late that night everyone sat together in the big drawing room at Woodcutter's mansion. There was the horrible stench of smoke hanging thick, even though thanks to favorable winds and a late afternoon downpour of rain, the house had been untouched by the fire. Will wearily wiped his eyes, spreading black soot all across his brow. The men were all filthy, but no one seemed to mind. Even the over-powering slave woman, Samantha, didn't mention the filthy footprints and sooty stains all through the house. Everyone just stared at the center of the room as if in a stupor. Louisa was crying quietly.

" 'Tis so hard to believe it. Seems like a horrible dream, and I pray I shall wake up ... but I can't. I wonder ... will it ever seem real to me?" Lucille turned questioning eyes that glistened with tears toward

Hannah as she continued. "How shall I live without him?"

Hannah wisely knew that her friend meant the question to be rhetorical. She left Will's side and simply put her arms around Lucille. She sobbed quietly against Hannah's shoulder.

"Mama, someone will have to send word to Little Marc," Karla choked on her brother's name.

"I already did," Duffy muttered, surprising all the adults that he'd taken the initiative. "As soon as . . . as they . . . uh, found . . . er . . . uh brought Uncle Marc's . . . uh. . . well, I rode into town and the new magistrate assured me that the note I gave him would be delivered to Little Marc and Emily afore noontime on the morrow. He was a ridin' up to the capitol with some word for one of the burgesses, so he'll deliver the note himself."

"Thank you, Duffy," Mistress Woodcutter said. "You know, after he'd been over to your place the other day workin' on the wagons he came home and said to me, 'That Freedom has turned into a man overnight.' I think he was right."

Tears filled Duffy's eyes. "He was the only one who always called me by my real given name."

"Oh, Papa, why did it have to happen?" a distressed Libby asked of Will. "First we lost Grandmother. And that was horrible enough. But she was old and . . . but why did Uncle Marc have to die?"

Will shook his head as if trying to clear his brain. "I don't know, Lib. And I doubt if we will ever know. All we know is that he was trying to get to the river probably hoping to wetdown some of the trees. Mayhap the smoke was too thick. Mayhap a branch or a tree fell on him. All we do know is that by the time the alarm got out and the men got here and into the woods to fight the fire . . . well, probably Marc was already . . ."

Even Will who usually was as solid as a rock couldn't make himself say the word.

Karla, who had ever been the strongest of the Woodcutter children picked up the narrative. She spoke gently to her grieving children. "What Uncle Will means to say is that by that time, Grandpa Woodcutter was already in heaven meeting Jesus and my little sister, Marta."

Mistress Woodcutter nodded bravely through her tears. "That's right, children. We must remember that your grandfather isn't hurting or anything. He's in heaven."

Just then Samantha came to the doorway. She was crying too. "They's some cold meat sandwiches and a pot of hot coffee on the sideboard in the dining room, iffen any of y'all wants it."

As if they were all puppets whose strings had been pulled, everyone arose.

"Chad, we should probably go on home," Will confided to Karla's husband. "Will you folks be staying with Lucille?"

"Oh, yes. And I think Daniel and Louisa will stay too. I can't tell you how we appreciate all you've done. I don't know if we'd e'er a gotten 'im laid out in there without you and Hannah's help."

"Oh, 'twas nothin'. I just wish . . . wish I'd a gotten here . . . oh, well. Hannah, shouldn't we start for home?"

Libby went upstairs to get the sleeping Willy. Everyone was reluctant to leave. Somehow staying together made their horrible loss more bearable. But knowing that eventually Lucille would crave solitude or just her family's nearness, the Stivers family wisely took their leave with promises to return on the morrow.

The trip home seemed long and quiet. Everyone was lost in his or her own memories of their friend and neighbor.

"We'll put off the trip to Ohio until spring," Will said authoritatively. "Lucille will need us, and 'tis probably too late to consider it for this year."

"Mayhap 'tis for the best," Hannah replied. "But we shall still go, won't we dear?"

"Yes," he replied. "We'll continue to make our plans. He would have wanted that. But the joy is all gone from the plannin', that's for certain. Suddenly I'm so weary."

"I'll do the horses, Pa," Duffy responded.

In bed that night once again Will and Hannah cried together.

"My lady, do you think we'll e'er understand why God allows things like this to happen?"

"Nay, I doubt it. But Will, 'tis important I think to remember that God *allows* it. But He never *causes* it!"

Both were silent for a while.

"He was a wonderful man, Will. Why, if he hadn't purchased me that horrible day when we first landed in America . . ."

"I was just thinkin' on the same thing. I wonder where any of us would be if it weren't for Marc Woodcutter. How I shall miss him! Other than you, my lady, he was my best friend."

Hannah patted Will's back as he put his head on her shoulder. Before long, with tears still wet on both their cheeks, they fell into an exhausted sleep.

Chapter 16

hanksgiving of 1771 came too closely on the heels of the fire. Hannah roasted a chicken and Libby baked pies, but when they asked Lucille to join them she wisely declined.

"Little Marc and Emily insisted on staying until after the holiday. We are all to go to Karla's for a meal of sorts, but no one feels like celebrating. You folks try to have a happy day though."

And try they did. They played the thankful game and choked their way through a song of praise after their quiet meal. But eventually they gave up. Each pursued his own particular hobby in the afternoon, deciding their loss somehow didn't seem so great if they kept busy.

On the second Sunday of December, Lucille spoke with Hannah after church. "Has Will determined when we will be leaving?"

Hannah hoped the surprise she felt in her heart did not register on her face. Could it be that Lucille was going to move to Ohio alone? She and Will had just assumed that Marc's untimely death would mean that they would be moving to the frontier without her. But now . . .

"Well, he feels we should wait for spring."

"Do you think he and Duffy can finish my wagon? I've almost decided exactly what I wish to take and what . . ."

Hannah could contain her joy no longer. She hugged Lucille. "Oh, Mistress, I never dreamed you'd still go with us since . . . since . . . without Marc. I cannot express to you how happy this makes me. Oh, come home and dine with us so's we can plan."

The Sunday before Christmas was when the children did the pageant at church. It was nearly identical from year to year, but no one tired of the ageless theme. This year was Duffy's last to perform. He was given the important part of King Herod. When the monarch told the Wise Men to "go and search diligently for the new King," one could have heard a pin drop in the sanctuary. Duffy's voice was so low and forceful that he made the performance very believable. Libby had no speaking part. But never was there a lovelier Madonna than the one played by her. As Hannah watched the performance, a gasp escaped her lips.

"Why, my little girl is a little girl no longer. She looks so lovely—and so mature. She looks much older than Karla did when she married Chad."

Then another thought came to Hannah. As Libby picked up the bundled doll which represented the Christ Child, Hannah realized that the Mother of the true Christ was probably not much older than Libby. Right then she made a decision. She could not hold back the sands of time so she might just as well move ahead.

The next day found Hannah at the mercantile purchasing several lengths of materials. Some were homespun, some calico, and there were a few nice woolens. If Libby could be that convincing in the part of Mary, it was indeed time that she lower her hemline to her ankles. All the material was to be kept hidden from Libby until Christmas, so she asked the storekeeper to wrap it all well. On a last minute whim, she picked up a paper of hairpins and the latest fashion in clips also. She chuckled as the storekeeper nodded.

"Ah, yes, Mistress Stivers. When the skirts go down, the hair goes up."

From behind her came a familiar low voice. "Mistress Stivers? Hannah, is it you?"

Turning around she nearly bumped into Captain Phillip Woodcutter.

"Captain! When did you dock?" He was still as handsome as ever in his uniform. Indeed, he looked spit-shined from head to toe. His blue eyes sparkled and his grin spread from ear to ear.

"I've only just landed this morn. I was on my way out to Marc's place, but decided I shouldn't go in both unannounced and empty-handed. What do you think? Shall I take them a ham? Or would something frivolous and unnecessary be ... Hannah! What is it? You're as white as your shirtwaist! What's wrong?"

She turned to the counter and picked up her purchases to hide her confusion. What should she say? She closed her eyes for the briefest second, sending an earnest prayer for wisdom to the Almighty.

"I'm all right, Phillip. Only do come outside with me, please."

"Hannah?" he questioned as she threw her purchases under the seat of the buckboard.

"Oh, Phillip," she began haltingly. "You don't know, do you? Several weeks ago there was a bad fire on the northern edge of Marc's land. You know the place. 'Twas that stand of walnut trees he had just planted when first I arrived here in Norfolk, all those years ago. We tried to reach you, Phil, but 'twas impossible. For the *Wedgewood* was at sea. Phil ..." her voice faltered.

He took hold of her arms and his grip was vise-like. "What happened?" he begged.

"Marc ... well, he's gone, Phil. He died in the fire

that night." As the tears spilled down his cheeks, Hannah continued. "No one knows exactly what happened. Whether he breathed too much smoke or was knocked out by falling limb. I . . . I'm so sorry, Phillip."

She wisely let him walk away for a brief spell. When he'd gained control of himself, he turned back and helped her up onto the seat of her wagon.

"How is Lucille? And . . . and the children? I . . . I just can't believe it. Why, I just got a letter from Little Marc when I came into port in which he told me his father had sold the company and was moving west with you folk. I was going to . . . but never mind. I suppose that's out of the question now. Where is Lucille? I should pay my respects."

"She's still out at their house. Marc's will set the servants free, but they won't leave her. So she's doing fairly well. Believe it or not, she is still going to move with us come spring. We're overjoyed by that decision, of course. But it did surprise us. She's held up as well as can be expected, Phil. Oh, I know she will be so glad to see you. Whyn't you go on out? And do come with Lucille to our place for Christmas, of course."

It was getting cold and snow began to fall as they spoke. Hannah continued, "How long are you in port, Phillip?"

He just shook his head. "That sort of depends, Hannah—on lots of different things.

As she gathered the reins, he looked up at her with such deep sorrow in his eyes that she felt her heart would break. "I'm glad I ran into you," he continued. "Thank you for telling me. I know it wasn't easy for you. But think how 'twould've been iffen I'd just gone a blusterin' in out at their place not knowing that my brother . . . he's . . ." He turned away. "We'll see you soon, Hannah," he mumbled as he mounted the rented steed and galloped away toward the Woodcutter mansion.

When all the hubbub of Christmas Day was over and only Will and Hannah sat staring into the dying fire, they both sighed at precisely the same moment. Then they smiled at each other contentedly.

" 'Twas a good day, wasn't it, my lady?"

"Oh, yes, darling. I think everyone had a good day— or at least as good as was possible for this year anyway. Thank you again for the material, dear. It is so beautiful."

"Mayhap 'twill be considered a bit extravagant on the frontier. But I just could not resist that beautiful shade of blue. Besides, I want you to still have some lovely things. Just because we are goin' to be livin' near the heathen Indians doesn't mean my lady has to dress like one."

"I think Libby was genuinely surprised by all her new skirts and dresses, don't you, Will?"

"Ah, yes, our Miss Liberty could ne'er have faked that look of shock. Mayhap she thought we were never going to allow her to grow up."

"And she certainly did look grown-up in the longer skirts and with her hair up, didn't she? I shall be afraid to let her out of my sight, what with all the redcoat soldiers a makin' their presence known around town."

"I've been meanin' to speak to you about that, my lady. I see no point in Lib going back to school anymore, do you? I mean, we'll be leaving afore the end of the term in the spring. And, well—mayhap 'tis just my father's heart a-worryin'. But I'd just feel better iffen she stayed here to home with us until we move."

Hannah patted him playfully on the arm. "I know exactly what you mean, Will Stivers. You saw the same looks of admiration on the faces of those rowdy big school boys as I did last Sunday when Libby played Mary in the pageant. It might surprise you to know I'd made the same decision about school. I know Lib won't give us any trouble about it either. I fear her heart still belongs to Little Marc."

Will nodded glumly. There was a comfortable silence for a while.

"I think Duffy was surprised with his gift also."

"Yes, I'm glad I went ahead and made the trade for the musket, though I fear what Libby will do when she finds out Jonah isn't out there in the barn any more."

"Don't worry so much, Will. Somehow I think growing up has taken the joy out of chasing that goat all over kingdom come for Libby."

"Willy looked so sweet when I put him to bed. He just would not let loose of that little wool doggy that Lucille brought to him. Isn't she somethin', Will? In the midst of all her own pain and sorrow, she was a thinkin' about all of us and makin' us gifts."

"Mayhap she found out like I did that the best way to get your mind off of your own loss is to think about other people."

"Oh, Will, I'm sorry. Sometimes I forget that it hasn't been that long ago for you either. Was it hard for you, not havin' your mother here today?"

"I can't deny 'twould've been nice to be able to spend one last holiday together. But the Lord knows best. And I wouldn't wish her back. She's in a much better place. With no coughing nor pain." His voice broke. "I miss her, of course. But I suppose in the long run 'tis for the best. The trip would've been awfully hard on her."

Hannah nodded thoughtfully. "Will, did it seem to you like Phillip was a bit preoccupied today? It's like his mind is somewheres else . . . afar off."

"Yes, I noticed it. Especially when Duffy asked him if he could go see the ship before he sailed. He paused so long before he answered that I thought for a minute he was going to make some momentous announcement. But then he just said, 'We'll see.' "

"I thought that even his saying that was so unlike

120

Phillip. He's always been willing to do 'most anything the children asked of him. Well, whatever his problem is, I have a feeling Lucille knows what it is and tried to help him cover it up. If you remember, 'twas right then, when Duffy asked about the ship that she decided they'd best move on if they wanted to get to Karla's and Louisa's yet this day to see the babies with their Christmas things."

"Now, my lady, don't go borrowing trouble or making a mystery where mayhap there ain't one. I imagine both Lucille and Phillip were a missin' Little Marc something awful today. 'Twas a shame he couldn't come home. Mayhap that's the ony reason they seemed distracted."

"Oh, I'm sure they missed him. He was always the Captain's favorite. Remember how he used to call him 'Little Phillip' by his middle name to tease. Yes, 'tis too bad they couldn't come but the letter Lucille got last week said Emily is dreadfully sick with bein' in the family way and all." She hesitated a bit. "No, Will, I'm sure there's something afoot. Neither Lucille nor the Captain acted normal."

Will rose and began to bank the fire. "Well, my lady . . . 'tis time to turn in. It has been a good many hours since William Justice announced the arrival of Christmas 'pessants' to us all."

They walked arm in arm into the bedroom.

"Merry Christmas, darling."

"And the same to you, my lady."

Several weeks passed quietly. The wagons were nearing completion. Libby and Hannah were finishing up the sewing that needed to be done before the trip. Everything was pointing to an early spring. Duffy had used his new musket to bring down a buck deer, several pheasants, and one wild goose. The meat hung in the smokehouse. When completely cured it could be packed in a large barrel which had been divided into sections to separate the different meats. Will checked his copy of the almanac repeatedly and it was decided that, barring any unforseen storms, the wagons would pull out in early April, right after Easter.

On March third, a knock was heard at the Stivers' front door. Hannah was busy with Libby upstairs sorting through bedding. She shouted down the stairwell, "Who is it?"

The voice that answered sounded happier than it had in months.

"The latchstring is out. C'mon in, Lucille. And c'mon upstairs. Lib and I are just trying to decide which bedding to take and which to give away. Lib seems attached to . . ."

But as Lucille entered the room, her countenance stopped Hannah mid-sentence.

Libby finally broke an awkward silence. "Aunt Lucille, what's come over you? Why, your face is shinin' with happiness so much that iffen you was Moses you'd have to hide it with a veil."

"Well, ladies," their friend began. "I have good news. You know how I've been dreading goin' off to the frontier alone. And I hadn't told you, but I'd also been dreadin' seein' Phil go back to the *Wedgewood*. His being around has helped to fill up all the long lonely hours so much."

"Lucille," Hannah interrupted, "you're not going out to the Ohio country alone. How many times must I tell you? You're goin' with us! And Will just said last night that iffen you'd be willin' when we get there we'd just build one extry big log house rather than two littler ones, and you can just live with us so's you won't have to be lonesome."

"Hannah, you don't understand. That's just it. I'm not goin' alone. Phillip and I were up half the night talkin'. Actually, that's the way it's been for several weeks. And he's out in the barn right now askin' yer

122

Will if it'd be all right with you'uns for him to sign on as a member of your wagon train."

The joke was lost on the incredulous Hannah. "The Captain? Why, what about the *Wedgewood?*"

"I know. I can't imagine it myself . . . but it seems Phillip came off this last voyage more tired of the sea than he'd e'er imagined. He had made up his mind that he wanted to retire and become a farmer. Said he's eat alive by rheumatiz and the sea air makes it so's he can hardly walk. But when he got here and heard about Marc . . . well, he just didn't say anything. The way we got started talking was when I said I hated to see him go back to the sea. Then he said he isn't going back to the sea. He sold the *Wedgewood* to the first mate afore he e'er came to see us. I guess the ship set sail right after the holidays."

Hannah said, "No wonder he was so evasive with Duffy on Christmas. But why did he keep it all a secret?"

"Well, he said he had lots of thinking to do. And then he wanted the timing to be just right. Hannah, you knew he went up to see Little Marc and Emily early in February?"

"Yes. How is she getting along?" Hannah asked with a sad glance at Libby who was quietly refolding the counterpane she had candlewicked last winter.

"Oh, I guess she's past the worst of it. But Hannah, do you know why Phillip went to see them?"

"I presumed to say goodbye for I figured he'd be sailing soon."

"No, Hannah . . . oh dear! I can't stand it any longer. Can't either of you guess why I am so happy?"

The mother and daughter stared, shaking their heads.

"Can't you see? He'd already spoken to Karla and Chad and Louisa and Daniel. I told him I couldn't do it unless I was sure all the children understood and

123

approved. It seemed too soon. But I guess if the town is scandalized by it, they should just try to understand that what would be wrong in some instances just isn't wrong in others."

"What are you talking about?" Libby asked impatiently.

Lucille's face turned as red as a pickled beet and her eyes glistened with tears. "Dear, dear friends—Phillip has asked me to be his wife."

Both the Stivers women squealed in delight and hugged Lucille. The tears spilled over and before long all three were drying their eyes.

"Wouldn't Uncle Marc be happy if he knew?" Libby said in a hushed tone.

"Oh, Libby, I feel certain that he does know. And yes, I'm quite certain he is happy!" her mother corrected.

"You don't think it is awful, then?" asked a relieved Lucille. "You know I should still be in mourning for nigh onto a year."

"Marcus wouldn't have wanted that. When will the wedding be?"

"Well, when Will decided he wanted to leave in early April, Phillip went straight to the vicarage. The bans will be read at services for the next two weeks. And we are to be wed in a small quiet ceremony there at the parson's house on Sunday a fortnight from now. Phillip was going to ask Will this morn to stand up with him as his best man."

From the kitchen the ladies heard Will shout, "Ho, ladies! Upstairs! Come down and drink a toast to the bride and groom."

The shout was immediately followed by a shriek and crying from the downstairs bedroom.

Libby intervened. "Oh, they've woke up Willy. You two go on. I'll care for the baby."

Amidst all the merriment of toasting with the highly taxed tea in the kitchen, the adults never knew that

124

Libby's tears mingled with little Willy's. Methodically she changed his diaper. But while she did, she grumbled to him.

"So Emily is feeling better? Well, I'm glad for her. I surely and purely am. But, oh, Willy—will there ever be a man for me?"

The still sleepy toddler lovingly held up his arms to his sister saying, "Wibby, Wibby!"

She held him to her bosom and cried.

Chapter 17

hillip and Lucille were married as planned in a quiet ceremony at the vicarage.

"Too quiet, iffen you'd ask me—which, of course, no one did!" growled Karla to Hannah. "I wanted to give them a big gala reception, so's to show to all the townsfolk that us children approve of Mama and Uncle Phil. But she would have no part of it. Made me solemnly promise not to do anything as a surprise either."

"Try to look at it from her point of view, dear," replied Hannah who was always the peacemaker. "She understandably feels a bit distraught over what people's reactions will be to the idea. I tried to tell her that her true friends won't care—will be happy for her, even."

"And I tried to tell her that she shouldn't care at all what other people would think. Maybe in one way it's good that you all will be headin' west soon, though I don't know how I shall ever manage." Karla's eyes filled with tears as she turned to put on her cape. "Remember the farewell dinner at our place on Easter."

The goodbyes were all said. The wagons were all packed. The houses were spotlessly waiting for their new owners. The goats had been sold. One cow was tethered to the rear of the supply wagon. Phil and Lucille, Will and Hannah, Duffy, Libby, and a very excited Willy stood in a tight circle in the Stivers' front yard holding hands.

"And dear Lord, we are just trusting that You will lead us to exactly the right spot to settle. You know our needs better'n even we do, Father . . . so as we set out on this journey we place ourselves in Your hand. Thankin' You in advance, Lord, in the name of Your son—Amen."

Everyone said "Amen" in unison except Willy who shouted " 'Men! Now go!" all in one breath. And so the trip began.

Will and Hannah were on the seat of the first wagon, with Libby trying to calm down Willy in the rear. Phil and Lucille had pulled their wagon in behind the Stivers'. Duffy brought up the rear driving the old buckboard. They headed north out of town on a path which took them right past the burned section of woods.

Lucille shed tears unashamedly and Phil just held her hand quietly. When her crying was spent, she turned to him. "I know it's hard for Hannah to leave here, too. There are the three crosses on the hill at the back of their land, or what used to be their land."

"Will's leavin' his mother's grave, also," Phil reminded her. "Let's hope the frontier will be kinder to us all."

" 'Tis certainly wondrous kind of them to be willin' to stop in just two days so's we can see Marc and Emily," she replied.

"Well, the trail leads so near to Williamsburg, 'twould hardly seem right not to stop."

A journey routine was quickly established which was to be observed the entire trip. They would follow the James River almost the entire way. Just next to the

127

river, there was always a stand of trees. But so many people had followed the river that just beyond the trees there was a path of sorts. So, at each nooning stop while Will or Phil built the fire, Libby would carry water from the river in the biggest kettle. This water would be used for coffee, if needed in cooking the vegetables, and what was left was for doing up the dishes. Duffy cared for the needs of the cow, both milking and leading her to the nicest grazing area. The women did the cooking. And everyone helped in keeping an eye on Willy.

Those first two days there was an almost carnival atmosphere among the travellers. They passed other folk, most of whom were heading into Norfolk for supplies.

"Where ya' headin?" the travellers would ask.

"Fer the frontier. The Ohio country," they'd respond.

"Best o' luck!"

"May the good Lord go afore ye."

"Hopin' ya make it with yer bells on," referring to the jinglers strung between the horses. These were sometimes stolen by road pirates at night so that the sleeping travellers would not be disturbed by the nervous horses when the robbery was taking place.

Hannah had a lot of time for silent 'woolgathering' as she had called it in her younger days. Each time someone passed and inquired about their destination, she noticed the pride in the voice of whoever called back the answer. "Mayhap," she thought, "this is our destiny, as Lucille said. Leastways, we'll be gettin' away from all the talk of the tea tax and quartering Redcoats." She didn't think she could bear it if Duffy ever had to go to war.

"Here's the cut-off up to Williamsburg," Will said interrupting her thoughts. "We're makin' real good time, my lady. If this continues, we'll be able to be all settled and have crops planted in good shape for this year."

As they came into Williamsburg, Hannah was taken aback by the grandeur of the city. It was similar in size to Norfolk, but it looked so much more permanent and ... and ...

"Mama, is everyone who lives here rich?" an awestruck Libby asked.

"These are probably the homes of the members of the House of Burgesses," Will answered. "See, the man in the yard there in his powdered wig and robe. There are probably some common ordinary homes farther in."

At a wide spot in the road near the town green, Phil's wagon passed the Stivers' and he shouted, "Follow me to where they live."

Several turns later the wagons were pulled round back and into the stable yard of the home Little Marc and Emily shared with Mrs. Brennan. It was late afternoon and Hannah was flustered by the impropriety of arriving unannounced near suppertime.

"Stuff and nonsense," the stooped little lady said, beaming a sincere welcome. "We've a big pot of stew, plenty for all. And Emily and I baked pies this morn while Marcus was in school."

Emily, excited about entertaining her in-laws, giggled. " 'Twas mostly Mardell did the baking. I'm just learning. I did roll out the dough," she said, but immediately blushed deeply hoping they wouldn't think she was bragging.

Little Marc patted her shoulder proudly. "She's learning to be a good cook. But it's getting harder and harder for her to get close to the table." Emily's pregnancy was indeed very evident.

"She even looks beautiful in those awful 'Mother Hubbards'," Libby thought. But somehow it was not with envy anymore. Her old longings for Little Marc were slowly fading into a beautiful memory. Now she just longed for someone to replace these feelings with current reality.

After a delicious meal, Mrs. Brennan retired to her room allowing the Stivers and Woodcutters use of the parlor. The evening was interspersed with laughter as old stories were resurrected.

"Has Emily ever heard about the time Duffy nearly froze chasing the goats?"

And the story of Will's mittens that became a baby sweater was recounted.

"Are you taking that sweater along, Aunt Hannah?" Little Marc asked.

"Oh my, yes. Not that I think there'll be any more babies to wear it. But that yarn is so precious I wouldn't want to e'er lose it. It's in the trunk on the buckboard Duffy's drivin'."

"If we're to get an early start, we'd best be goin' to bed," Will said, rising as he spoke.

"I wish there were rooms for all of you," Emily said.

"No, dear. We'll just sleep in the wagon, with Duffy and Will beneath as we shall every night," Hannah responded.

"Mama, you and Uncle Phil can have the guest room. Mardell said to insist."

The next morning after a quick breakfast, Little Marc and Emily stood waving as the wagons pulled away. There were tears flowing freely or else just beneath the surface for everyone.

"Gd'bye, Lib. Be happy!" Little Marc shouted, as he named each person in his farewells.

"I shall!" responded the young woman bravely. "And I know your baby will be beautiful, Em. I hope I get to see it some day."

Will and Hannah exchanged a look of surprise. "Mayhap 'twas a good thing we stopped here in Williamsburg after all. Unless my ears are deceiving me, that girl of ours has done some more growin' up in just the last fifteen hours or so," Will said as the wagons rolled out of town.

They were following the James again. The land was rolling right near the river. The days were uneventful, but before anyone had a chance to grow bored they began to see many wagons and traffic as they neared Richmond. The third afternoon out from Williamsburg they camped amidst several other travellers in a locust grove just outside the city.

Will and Phillip went into the city to buy the supplies they needed. Axle grease for the wagons was already running low. Will may have been guilty of over-greasing the wagons, but he was determined they should spare the horses any undue strain. The women went to the river bed and washed clothing while the men did the shopping. By the time all had assembled again, it was a late supper and off to bed.

As they undid their bed rolls under the wagon Duffy spoke.

"Papa, was there any important news in Richmond?"

"I'm presumin' yer meanin' news of the ever brewin' conflicts betwixt the colonies and old Mother England? Well, nothing any different than what you were hearing from yer friends back in Norfolk. Oh . . . they did do what they called a burnin' in effigy here one day last week, I guess."

"What's that?"

"Well, it seems this here one merchant in town is known to be a loyalist. Guess he was always spouting off 'bout lovin' England. And he also tried to push the English tea on his customers, makin' 'em pay the stupid tax and all. Well, it seems some boys—mayhap the Sons of Liberty, but no one's saying—well, they made a stuffed dummy of the man, wrote his name on a sign under him, hung this dummy by the neck and burned it. The man I bought the axle grease from said the merchant hasn't opened his store since."

"Y'know Papa—that's the only reason I'm sorry we're moving now. I would have loved to join those

Sons of Liberty. I think some day there will be a war for independence."

"Yer probably right there, son. But we'll have us a different kind of war to worry over on the frontier— breakin' virgin sod and watchin' for Indians."

Inside the wagon, Hannah interrupted Willy's lullaby to eavesdrop on this conversation. She sighed as she prayed silently, "Thank you, Lord, that we're getting Duffy out of civilization before he got involved with all these rebels. No matter how bad the Indian menace is, I shall always be less afraid of them than I was of talk of revolution." It was a prayer Hannah would often remember in years to come.

* * * * * * * * * * * *

"Mama, I'm tired of the James. It seems like we've been followin' it forever," Libby complained two weeks later. They had been going uphill on such a steep incline today that at mid-morning the ladies had disembarked to lighten the load the horses pulled. Lucille, Hannah, and Libby walked together with Willy running ahead a spell, then wanting to be carried.

Lucille said, "I'll take a turn," as she scooped up the toddler. "I know what you mean, Lib. This James is the meanderingist river I ever did see. Seems like it would've been a lots quicker route to just point the horses at them foothills up yonder we been seein' fer days and forget the river."

Hannah corrected. "Oh, no. What would we have done for water? And the few people we've seen have all been because of the river. I know it weaves around, but Will said we are better off to stick to its course than our own.

"What are they the foothills of, Mama?"

Hannah looked confused.

"You know," the young lady continued. "To be real

foothills they have to be the foothills of some mountain range. What are the mountains called?"

Just then they heard splashing as a horse trotted right through the shallow James and stopped short at Will's wagon. Duffy cracked the whip over the mule pulling the buckboard so's to come alongside and hear the news, as did Phillip. Libby pulled up her skirts and sprinted up to the men just as the rider was about to go on. It seemed he was on his way from Bedford to Charlottesville with an urgent message of an illness for a relative. Though Duffy had questioned him about the rebellion, he seemed not to know or care.

"Excuse me, sir—" said Liberty.

"Yes, Ma'am," he said with obvious admiration in his voice. "What can I do for you, my lady?"

Libby blushed furiously. No one had ever treated her as a grown-up or called her "ma'am" before.

"What is the name given to the mountains off in the distance?"

"They are officially called the Appalachians, ma'am. But folks here about all calls 'em the Blue Ridge Mountains 'cause it always looks bluish up on the ridge."

"And on the other side of 'em?"

"The other side? Why, accordin' to yer Daddy that's where yer headin'. There's been lots of disputing about whether it belongs to Virginny or Pennsylvania. But fer the time bein', everything on the other side of them Blue Ridge Mountains exceptin' Kentucky is called Ohio!"

Chapter 18

rom then on, the ladies walked a lot. The foothills fell away and the ascent became steeper. After they'd crossed the first really steep mountain, they camped in a lovely valley. In the morning as they prepared to leave, a big, red-haired man rode into their camp bareheaded.

"And where do ye folks be headin' on this fine morn?" he asked in a thick Scottish brogue.

"We're on our way to the Ohio frontier," Will replied.

"Sure and ye don' wanna be bringin' this fine family o' yourn into all those Indian scares. Ye look like such fine outstandin' folk. Whyn't ye think on turnin' off here and followin' this fine valley and me? We'll lead ye to the fine town of Fincastle. There's some as are startin' ta call it Botetourt Court House 'causin' they're hopin' we'll be named the county seat. O'course, that's if we get enough settlers. Would y'all be interested?"

Hannah, who had already climbed up into the huge wagon, found herself silently hoping. "Yes, oh, yes. We'd be more than interested. We'd love to follow you to where there are other people settled and a real community growing." She hadn't realized until this very minute how bone-weary she'd grown. But even as her heart hoped desperately that Will would consider the big Scotsman's idea, her ears heard this reply.

"We thank you, sir. We certainly do. But we've all got our hearts set on livin' out where there'll be no neighbors encrouchin' on our lands. And so, we'll move on as planned. Good day to you, sir."

"Excusin' me . . . but if I cain't get ye to consider our town, at least be lettin' me give ye some friendly advice. I'm guessin' yer followin' the James River here?"

"Yes," Will replied as he climbed up on to the wagon seat and picked up the reins.

"Well, just up ahead, over those next hills, there be a fork in the river. If ye follow the south fork, it'll put ye in a nice peaceful lookin' valley. And the river flowin' nice and calm like. But there hain't no easy way outten that valley. Them old Blue Ridges rise up on all sides of ye, nearly straight up! On t'other hand, the north fork looks wicked. The river is cut deep, into a fearsome gorge. And the water is mostly white rapids. But just ta the right side of the gorge is a level, easy way fer wagons. Ye'll follow it 'bout a day and then there'll be a natural bridge across the river. Cut out of solid rock, like God knew people'd wanta cross there ta get over ta the levels a Greenbriar."

"Is the bridge safe? Will it hold our wagons?"

"Oh, 'tis safe all right. But there's some hain't got the inner fortitude to try crossin'. Ye'll be seein' what I'm meanin' when ye get there."

"And these levels of . . . of, what did you say?" Phillip interrupted. "What are they?"

"O' the Greenbriar! She's the purtiest river in these parts. The levels run straight west for prob'ly a day and a half's trip fer yer wagons. Nice easy rollin' hills. Ye'll be all surrounded by the purtiest mountains—purtiest country this side o' Scotland."

"And then?" Will was thinking that this man must

have been sent straight from God. For once they'd passed the source of the James, he'd had no idea how they were to proceed. He hoped he could remember all these directions and once again was thankful for Phillip's presence on the journey. But the man was continuing his narrative.

"After ye've passed through the levels, ye'll come to the Greenbriar. Ye cross over her and follow her south a ways to what's called Culbertson's Bottom. There ye'll swing north and west 'long the New River and in a few days ye'll be outta the mountains. From then on, yer on yer own. Fer I've ne'er been comfortable on flat land. Iffen I cain't see the mist risin' off the hills of a mornin', I gets so homesick fer Scotland thet I cain't stand it.

There was a long pause. Then Will said, "Well, sir, ... I expect we'd better be startin' out. I don't know how I can e'er thank you for all your advice."

The big Scot grinned. "What are neighbors for, iffen not to help? May God go with ye." And turning his big bay mare, he quickly rode away.

The wagons pulled into line and started on their weary way. "Can it be that if that man is right ... and my calculations are correct ... do we have only about another week to go?" Hannah asked.

Libby poked her head through the sun-bleached canvas at precisely that moment to ask who that man was. But she forgot her question when Will gave his answer.

"One more week!" she shouted joyously. And she and Willy proceeded to make a sing-song game of it which was often repeated over the next several days.

"One more week. Less than a fortnight to go! Only one more week, till we'll be in O-hi-o!"

The Scotsman's surveillance of the land proved accurate every bit of the journey. By mid-morning of the day they talked with him, they were following the north fork of the river. They stopped for an early lunch and to fill the water barrels. As yet, the barrels had seemed so unnecessary for they had followed the river so closely it had been their constant source of water. But here, as predicted, the wagons were beginning a steep ascent ever farther above the river bed.

"Willy, you must hold on to Libby's hand every step of the way," Hannah shouted from the wagon seat, when they were rolling again.

The child was so curious and did not appear to be a bit frightened of the steep cliff. Finally, to Libby's relief, he grew tired of walking and she passed him up to sit beside Duffy on the buckboard.

Late that afternoon, Willy was napping between Mama's trunk and Lucille's spinning wheel in the buckboard when Duffy shouted.

"Look, Papa! Up ahead! There's the natural bridge the man spoke about!" With anxiety in his voice, he continued. "Are we gonna ... gonna cross over that?"

'Twas nearly sundown when they came to the east end of the awesome span of rock which had created the natural bridge. Everyone disembarked the wagons and stood staring down into the chasm at the fast-flowing river below. The ground where they stood was even with the treetops of oaks and maples which had stood since time began.

"Oh my!" Lucille whispered with her hand over her mouth. When her gaze locked with Hannah's there was utter terror in both their eyes. Rolling her eyes toward Libby and Willy with a slight shake of her head, Hannah spoke.

"Isn't it beautiful? And how kind of that Scotsman to direct us this way! When shall we go over, Will?" Try as hard as she might, her voice still broke with fear.

Even the men were dumbstruck by the horror of crossing this smooth span of rock. Visibly shaking himself into action, Will answered.

"Well, like I always say, there's no time like the present. Let's get us across afore nightfall and then have a good big supper." Turning away from the women with a carefully guarded look in his eyes, he spoke again. "What do ya think, Phil? I say we walk the women and Willy across first so's they can be starting the dinner fire."

Immediately picking up the idea that Will did not want their families riding in the wagons across the precarious-looking rock, Phillip responded in kind.

"Yes, that's a good idea. How's about if I carry you, Master William Justice?"

It wasn't such a long span. It just seemed so confoundingly high!

"Don't look down, my lady. Just think of the other side," Will encouraged though the hand with which he supported Hannah's elbow shook a little.

Libby walked alone, a few paces behind her parents, and a few ahead of Lucille and Phillip, who was giving Willy a ride on his shoulders.

"Me up high," the toddler squealed.

The entire party inched their way across. Once he was confident they were going to make it, Duffy turned away from his vantage point to turn down the blinders on both horses and the mule. He changed the cow's tether from the rear corner to the center rear of the buckboard, thanking God for the hundredth time this trip that they did not have the goats to deal with.

As the walkers neared the other side, there was a place where the natural bridge narrowed. Sensing everyone's anxiety and with characteristic maturity, Libby glanced back at the baby.

"Let's sing our new song, Willy!"

And so they walked off the bridge on to solid ground again to the made-up tune of "Only one more week till we'll be in O-hi-o!"

At her father's instructions, Libby took the child in

her arms over to a nearby meadow. Standing on tip-toes, she could still clearly view the bridge. But Willy was romping around in the new spring grassland oblivious to the danger the wagons were about to en-counter.

Hannah grabbed Will's arm. "Oh, darling, I cannot see how the wagons will make it. Mayhap there is another way."

Kissing her lightly, Will gently pushed her away. "Don't fear, my lady. We'll do it one wagon at a time. The Lord will watch out for us. He knows our needs."

And so, the two women stood trembling and pray-ing as they watched their men slowly but surely bring the wagons across. Will's horse never stopped once. A mountain goat could not have been more sure-footed. Within minutes, the Stivers' wagon was pulled safely to the edge of the clearing where Libby cared for Willy.

"C'mon Phil," Will shouted. "Just keep her in the middle and you'll do fine." So with a shout of "Haw, Lizzie, Haw!" and a light crack of the whip, the second wagon pulled out onto the bridge. Lizzie was a younger mare and more skittish. She stopped in the middle of the bridge and took a faltering step back-wards and to the left, but Phil cracked her rump hard and in a brief moment she too had pulled her load safely across. Phil drove directly into the meadow and was tethering both the horses when Will shouted again.

"C'mon son. It's your turn now, You'll do just fine," he encouraged.

The mule took several faltering steps onto the bridge. Too late Duffy realized that he'd done nothing to blind the old cow to all that lay below. The usually docile animal began to dance back and forth bawling furi-ously. About halfway across the mule planted itself stock still as only a mule can do.

Duffy whipped the animal repeatedly, all the while talking quietly to the terrified cow.

"C'mon Bossy. It's just a bridge. Be still, won't you please?" But the rear of the wagon thrashed back and forth.

"Pa, help! He won't move! What shall I do?"

Without so much as a glance downward, realizing Duffy was in trouble, Will went out onto the bridge as quickly as his crippled gait allowed.

"Throw me the reins, son. I'll lead him. You go back to the back of the wagon and try to quiet Bossy."

By now Phillip had picked up a tiring Willy and carried him to the precipice. Libby, Hannah, and Lucille stood tightly squeezing each other's hands and mentally begging the animals to cooperate.

At last Will got the stubborn mule to begin to pull forward again. With Duffy holding the tether tight so the cow's head was over the tailgate of the buckboard and talking gently to Bossy, all appeared to be going well. But then they reached the spot where the bridge narrowed. Because the mule had turned a bit off course, the right rear wheel of the wagon went over the edge of the bridge.

Instinctively, Duffy jumped to the side of the wagon still on the rock, letting go of the tether as he did so. The cow thrashed furiously and managed to get her hind quarters over the side. Everyone screamed at the same time. Amidst all the hubbub, Duffy's eyes caught the action of his father cutting the mule's harness. He said later that all he heard was Will screaming, "Jump, Freedom, jump!"

Duffy landed flat on his face and stomach and lay there trembling as he heard the awful bellows of the cow falling away below the bridge. Tears began at the wrenching sound of the wooden wagon breaking apart on the rock outcroppings below.

Soon he felt the hands of Phillip helping him to his feet. Shakily, he led him off the bridge into the arms of his weeping mother. "Duffy, dear, are you . . .?"

Furious with himself, and wiping his eyes on his sleeve, he pushed out of her arms and went to where Will was trying to bring the rearing mule under control.

"Papa, I . . . I'm so sorry. I don't even know what happened. Guess . . . guess I'm not man 'nough for this job after all. How will we . . .?"

But his father just turned to him with such love on his face, the awful guilt was immediately gone. "Duff, 'twasn't your fault. Don't feel so badly, son. I couldn't have done any better. I'm just glad yer safe. As fer the supplies . . . God must have knowed we didn't need that stuff. It's over, boy. Now forget it."

As his father spoke, Duffy forced himself to go to the cliff and look down. There were bits and pieces of the wagon all down the rock side. Aunt Lucille's spinning wheel was shattered as were the barrels of meat. True, they were nigh empty by now; but the barrels themselves would have been such a help on the frontier. His new Christmas musket had been under the seat of the buckboard. And there, on the first big outcropping just below them, was the remains of Mama's trunk. It was all broken, like a giant had stomped on it. The dishes she had so lovingly packed were shattered too. From this distance, they looked like a doll's toys. Duffy's shoulders heaved with sobs.

"C'mon son," said his father as he led him back to the others. "We've much to be thankful for. Those were just *things!* We still have each other."

"But . . . Bossy!" Duffy sobbed.

"At least we can be thankful she hit the water and not the rock," Will stated matter-of-factly in a weary voice. "Now let's go help with supper."

When at last the camping dishes (which thankfully were packed in the boot of the Woodcutter's wagon) were all done and the sun was nigh down, Will suggested an early bedding down so's they could get a fresh start in the morning. In actuality, the tension of the crossing had left them all exhausted, so everyone agreed.

Duffy tossed and turned. His bedroll had never seemed so uncomfortable, but, of course, he now had bruises from the fall. Sometime near morning, a bright, full moon broke through the clouds.

"Why, it's nigh as bright as noonday," Duffy thought. And that's when the plan hit him. Silently, he rolled out from under the wagon and crawled to the edge of the clearing. Then he sprinted to the cliff where the accident had taken place.

When the first rays of dawn were streaking the sky, Will arose to begin the day. Not wishing to alarm Hannah, he went to the Woodcutter's wagon where Phil was preparing coffee. "Phillip, have you seen Duffy?"

"No, I thought you were all still asleep."

"Duffy's bedroll was way out from under the wagon. He's nowhere to be found."

"Mayhap he's off in the edge of the woods. When first I rise, I always need to . . ."

"Will, where's Duffy?" Hannah interrupted.

"Uh . . . I'm not sure, my lady. I only just got up myself."

From the edge of the clearing they heard a characteristic whistling. Relieved, they all turned toward the spot.

"What on earth . . .?"

"I wanted to bring more, Mama. But a lot of it was ruined. And . . . and I tried to think . . . what could I carry and . . . what would mean the most to you. Uncle Phillip, I'm sorry, but the cliff was too steep. I couldn't get to anything belongin' to you or Aunt Lucille. Here, Mama. I'm sorry I couldn't get more." Looking exhausted from the speech and his night's escapades, he gave his mother a bundle of things all tied up in his own jacket.

142

As she opened the pack, Hannah cried out in delight. He had salvaged her new blue dress, made from the Christmas material, and two of Libby's new long skirts. Wrapped carefully inside these were two of her fine china teacups and her old copper teakettle. With tears in her eyes, remarking about the cups not being broken, she lovingly placed the jacket around Duffy's shoulders.

"I almost forgot. I couldn't imagine us going on without this. It . . . it . . . well, I think I've heard the story so often . . . it's just a real important part of my life."

With the explanation, he handed her the wondrously fine snow white mitten sweater.

"Oh, Duffy . . . oh . . . thank you, son," she said with a sob.

Chapter 19

fter experiencing the loss of
the wagon the rest of the trip
had been, as Will described it,
"as easy as rolling off a log."
They lived through one hor-
rible day of a torrential downpour of rain while on the
levels of Greenbriar. But the women were thankful, for
the fresh rainfall they collected in the few remaining
pots and kettles made their hair feel wondrous soft
when they used it for shampooing. They'd laid over a
day in the levels while the womenfolk did laundry and
the men went hunting. Relaxed and refreshed, they
pressed on and reached the place known as Puckett's
Ferry on the evening of the next day. A long rope was
stretched across the lovely, lazy Greenbriar. At the end
of the rope in a tree hung a huge dinnerbell. Will
stepped to the tree and held Willy up so he could reach
the bell. The little boy rang it for all he was worth.

Across the river, a man came running out of a long,
log home. As he ran to the river's edge, the setting sun
glistened off his bald head. He was pulling suspenders
higher onto his shoulders as he ran. At the edge of the
river, he shouted.

"Be ye wantin' to cross the Greenbriar?"

"Yes, we've two wagons. Seven people, one of them a child. Two horses, one mule," Phillip shouted back. "How much?"

Once the price had been agreed upon, the man made a raft appear as if by magic. It has been hidden behind shrubbery at the river's edge. Mr. Puckett brought the barge-like raft across the river quickly by walking from the back of the craft to the front always moving his hands one over the other on the rope. When he reached their shore, he shook hands with Phillip, Will, and Duffy.

"Puckett's the name, and ferryin's my life's work," he grinned. "and I've news for yer lady folks. Bein's as ya arrived here jist in time for supper, my little wife is goin' to insist that ya take vittles with us."

The crossing was uneventful, "nothing like when we last crossed water," Duffy thought. But neither his nor Libby's hearts could remain down for long in the wake of Uncle Phillip saying for all the world to hear, "Seven people—one of 'em a child." Did they actually appear fully grown to folks?

The food set out by Mrs. Puckett was a feast fit for kings. While they were eating their fill, the ladies remarked about how good food tasted when you didn't have to prepare it yourself. Afterward their little hostess went into her pantry. She returned with a walnut carrot cake in one hand and a cream pie in the other. Groans from all around the table were soon replaced by more delightful, conversation and lip-smacking sighs of contentment. This dear old couple was childless, but they lovingly adopted each stranger who used their ferry. The travellers enjoyed their fireside until late into the evening. At long last, when they went out to their wagons, it was with the promise of a big country breakfast in the morning before they moved on.

Their evening with the Pucketts had accomplished more than just good fellowship. Some of the carefully guarded money that Will and Phillip had brought with them had been used to purchase seed grains and potatoes, since they'd lost all their supplies at the bridge. The men breathed a sigh of relief after Mr. Puckett sold them what they needed at a good price. Now they could go on without the worry they'd been nursing since the accident.

Culbertson's Bottom land led the travellers alongside yet another river, this one called the New River. When they emerged from the Blue Ridges onto a wide stretch of prairie land, Duffy was the first to speak. He was riding the mule next to Will's wagon when he said,

"Papa . . . do you reckon . . . er, are we in Ohio?"

"Well, son . . . seein's as I can't seem to see no more mountains . . . and not even much in the way of hills out ahead of us . . . I think we probably are."

That evening they camped at a spot where a little creek emptied into the New River. Supper was over and Libby had just washed her hair. She sat with a purple knitted shawl around her shoulders, brushing the waist-length ebony curls and hoping the thick hair would dry before bedtime. The three men had walked down the creek, looking for a fording site. Hannah was in their wagon getting Willy into bed. Lucille had made up their bed and was just descending from the wagon when she saw a stranger on the other side of the fire. He was a young man and he stood completely still. There was a pail in his hands. His expression was of such rapture as he watched Libby that, rather than being frightened, Lucille was amused. She made herself cough to purposely interrupt his reverie.

"Oh, beggin' yer pardon, Ma'am," said the sandy-haired man blushing furiously. "My brother, Ruben, was hunting this afternoon and saw you folks makin' camp on our creek. So my mama said that I should bring this fresh pail of milk out to y'all fer yer supper." The entire statement had been made without his once

146

taking his eyes off Libby.

Just then the men returned and Hannah came down from their wagon. Introductions were made all around to Samuel Kelly ... "but folks jist call me Sam."

Libby stared at him, smiling, as she continued to brush her long curls. The men explained to Sam why they were there and found out that their judge of an easy spot to ford Kelly's Creek was indeed correct.

He kept hoping he would have the opportunity to speak directly to this vision of loveliness, but the men kept him engaged in conversations about the area.

" 'Bout an hour's ride from here is a wondrous bottomland jist sittin' there awaitin' on someone to farm it, Mr. Stivers. It's watered on one side by the New and t'other by the Elk River. I was gonna try farmin' it myself some day, but our pa jist died not long ago, so I guess I'll be livin' right here on the home place. Ruben, he ain't much of a farmer. But thet piece of propitty I was speakin' on. Iffen you'd like it, I could sell it to y'all. I ..." and here he turned to stare at Libby again ... "I think I'd like having y'all fer neighbors."

Neighbors! Will cringed at the word, even as Hannah and Lucille began to hope again.

"Are there other folk settlin' around here?"

"Well, no, sir. Actually, most of 'em are formin' up a town 'bout two days' ride away where the New and Elk join to become the Kanahwa River. That's a Indian name. Where the Kanahwa empties out of the Ohio, there's the town site. They call it Point Pleasant."

"Aren't we in Ohio then?" Duffy asked dejectedly.

"Most folks calls it Ohio. Some says Western Virginny. Whichever, it shore 'nuff is unsettled frontier."

Will sighed from relief, the ladies from despair. If it was two days' ride to a town, surely they'd be free of near neighbors and free to live as they chose for years to come.

"We'll take a look at the piece you're speaking of

147

tomorrow, Sam. Where can we find you?"

Again with a significant glance toward Libby, he stated, "Oh . . . I'll be around, sir. But . . . now I'd better git or Ma'll send Ruben out lookin' fer me."

Everyone said goodnight to the stranger.

"Mr. Kelly, do you want your bucket?" Libby asked. "I can empty the milk into . . ."

"Oh no," he responded. "I'll get it when I come to see yer Pa 'bout the land. G'night Miss."

"Goodnight, Mr. Kelly."

"That's Sam!" he shouted over his shoulder, as he sprinted for home. He never stopped until he reached the clearing where he shared the cabin with his ma and Ruben.

Dousing his head in the bucket by the door and rubbing furiously with the flour sack towelling, he entered the door and said, "Ma, I took the milk to the travellers. Real nice folk. Two families actually. One name of Stivers . . . other Woodcutter. They might be interested in buyin' the propitty."

He threw the towel onto the table and started up the ladder into the loft. "I think I'll go on up ta bed. Get an early start on the bean field thet away. Maybe I kin get it done before I go talk to Mr. Stivers about the land." He added as an afterthought. "Oh, Ma, by the way, I met the girl tonight that I'm goin' ta marry. She don't know it yet, but one fine day Liberty Stivers is goin' ta be Mrs. Sam Kelly. G'night, Ma!"

The Widow Kelly sat dumbfounded, shaking her head.

* * * * * * * * * * *

Just as Sam predicted he and Libby were wed. A circuit-riding preacher was passing through. He stayed with the Stivers on Thursday night, and on Friday at noon the wedding took place. There were no elaborate preparations. The bride and groom simply wore their best clothes, stood before him, and said "I do." He

148

prayed and then he was on his way. It was a year almost to the day after they had first met. So much had happened in that year.

"I wonder if I'll ever get used to havin' a different last name from you, Mama," Libby said as the four women sat quilting a month after the wedding.

The Widow Kelly interrupted. "It's a fine new last name ya've got, Libby. We're fearsome proud to have you in the family. My Sam, he thought you was never goin' to say yes to him."

"Well, 'twas just that there was so much work to do on our place. Even with Sam and Ruben helping all they could, it seemed to take forever to get the two cabins and the barn raised. I got so tired of living in that little lean-to with the branches of leaves for a roof!"

Everyone smiled, remembering. The women were seated around a tumbling-block patterned quilt in Sam and Libby's new little one-room cabin. They'd lived with Mrs. Kelly for the first three weeks of their marriage, so Libby was still quite excited over being hostess in her own home.

"You all just keep quilting. I'm going to make us some tea."

Lucille spoke thoughtfully. "A mightly lot has happened in a short length of time. And our Liberty has grown up so quickly. Just think ... in a couple more months little Willy will be three years old. I remember the day he was born like it was yesterday."

"I remember you told me that when you tried to get Libby to help you quilt that day, she rebelled." Hannah laughed, teasing her newlywed daughter. "I wonder what your Sam would think if he knew what a precocious tomboy you used to be."

Her mother-in-law jumped to Libby's defense. "Why, I doubt he'd believe it. He tells me every day how he can't believe that his little wife is only fourteen years old. He says she is so mature and such a good cook and such a seamstress and . . ."

"Enough!" Libby demanded. "I shall get a big head on me for sure. And besides, I'm almost fifteen!"

All too soon the sun was setting, and it was time for Hannah and Lucille to head for home.

"Let Willy stay all night, Mama. He's fallen asleep there amidst his blocks. I'll bring him home in the morning."

And so Hannah and Lucille climbed up into the new sidesaddles their husbands had brought them from the trading post.

Mrs. Kelly walked across the clearing to cook supper for Ruben, leaving Libby with her memories as she waited on Sam.

"Could I ever have been so young?" she wondered, remembering her heartbreak over Little Marc. She could not imagine life with anyone but Sam.

That evening she tried to express her thoughts after getting Willy tucked into the trundle.

"Sam, do you think our lives are planned out in advance by God? I mean, what if I'd been dumb enough to say no to your proposal one too many times, and you'd never asked me again?"

"I knew it was a sense of responsibility to see your folks settled that kept you refusing me. You loved me from that first night, just like I did you."

"Oh, Sam," she blushed. "Answer my question. Do you think God plans it all . . . and could we mess up His plan?"

Seeing she was serious, Sam grew thoughtful. "Well, Lib, I think it's like this. God has a perfect plan for us and I think He leads us through circumstances around us to fulfill a . . . a kind of destiny."

"But, what if we mess it up by not following His leading?"

"Well, we ain't God's puppets. That's for sure. He gives us a mind of our own and feelings. I don't know

150

if unhappiness is a result of not findin' our destiny or not fulfillin' His plan. I guess it's just our job to try our best to follow Him and He'll put us back on track somehow if we're tryin'."

"Wonder what *our* destiny is, Sam?"

"Well, I don't rightly know. But yer brother, Duffy—him and me was talking one day when we was fellin' the trees fer this cabin. He was a tellin' me all about some yarn yer Mama was given away back in Germany and how he rescued somethin' called a mitten sweater from the busted-up wagon at the Natural Bridge. I'll ne'er fergit what he said that day. His eyes was shinin' so bright, you know—how they do when he's real sincere. And he said, 'Sam, I think my mama and papa named me Freedom 'cause that is their destiny in life. To find true Freedom. Sam,' he said, 'I've ne'er seen my papa happier then he is here in this valley. Seems to me like happiness for him must be knowin' that their destiny of searchin' for freedom has now been fulfilled.' "

Chapter 20

n the spring of 1774, Hannah and Lucille were working together planting peas in their big garden. It had been decided that since their homes stood just across a small clearing from each other, there was no reason to plant two gardens.

" 'Twill be just one to weed, to cultivate, and to keep the deer and 'coons out of," Hannah had said proposing the idea to Will.

"Besides, you and Lucille won't have to shout when you talk to each other. I ne'er did see two women that never run out of anything to talk about like you two," he chuckled.

Hannah straightened up between the rows to rub her aching back. Glancing at her friend, she asked, "Lucille, what is it? Why, you're white as a ghost . . . and shaking like a leaf."

All Lucille could do was point. There at the edge of the forest stood a nearly naked red man. His hair hung to his waist in greasy braids and his face was painted with bright blue and yellow streaks.

"Oh, land sakes, it's just an Indian. You'd ought to be used to them by now. Why, we see canoes full of them pass our cabin 'most every day. Will has even traded some things with them. He says they're just curious about our ways when they stand and stare like that. He's probably just wondering what we're planting." All this was said without any more than the initial glance at the man. "Lucille, don't stare. Will says if we ignore them, they will ignore us."

"But the paint on his face! Is it . . . could it be war paint?"

By the time Hannah turned to get a second glance, the man had disappeared into the forest as silently as he'd come.

"Never mind. Let's just finish the peas afore the men are in from the fields for nooning," Hannah instructed. She tried to get her friend's mind off the savage by wondering aloud if Emily's baby was a boy or a girl. But she saw that Lucille's movements were still slow and shaky.

"Hannah, . . . I don't know if I just got overly fearful or what. But my head is swimming . . . I don't . . . feel . . ."

By the time Hannah had run the length of the row Lucille had collapsed. When she reached her side and felt her forehead, she realized the trembling was caused by fever as well as fear.

Just as Hannah was trying to decide how to lift her friend, she heard the men coming from the field behind Phillip and Lucille's cabin.

"Willy! Willy!" she shouted.

The robust little three-and-a-half-year-old came running from the cabin.

"Go get Papa and Uncle Phil," she said, pointing to where she could now just see the wagon at the edge of the far field. "Tell them to come quick. Aunt 'Cille is sick. Run fast!"

Within a short time they had Lucille in bed and Hannah was brewing camomile tea. She'd aroused from her swoon, but was still afire with fever. For the next several days, Hannah stayed day and night with the Woodcutters. Not only did Lucille lose everything she fed her, she developed a deep, dry cough. Mrs. Kelly came to help Hannah administer a mustard plaster.

"It's the ague, Miz Stivers. I've seen it afore. It took my husband to glory. Only a miracle can save this woman if the vomit e'er turns black in color."

Phillip walked the floor day and night, leaving all the farm work to Will and Duffy.

"He's useless here, darling." Hannah pleaded with Will to take Phillip to the fields during one of the brief breaks she allowed herself from her friend's bedside. They walked in the clearing to give the tired nursemaid fresh air.

"But my lady! he's even more useless in the fields. He just stands and wrings his hands. To tell the truth, Hannah, though I know now's not the time I should be complainin', Phillip isn't really much of a farmer. Every time a boat goes by on the river, I see the same longin' in his eyes."

But their conversation was cut short by the Widow Kelly emerging from the cabin. She shook her head forlornly as she showed the contents of the washbasin she carried to Hannah. The sputum was black.

They buried Lucille the next afternoon. Unbeknown to the others, Duffy had fashioned a coffin out in the barn just like he had for his grandmother. Will read the Scripture passage from the fourteenth chapter of John's Gospel, exactly as he had at the funeral of another Woodcutter some twenty-two years earlier. Hannah was almost stoical in her grief. She'd lost the dearest friend she had. Libby sobbed openly, and as they walked away from the little knoll she leaned against Sam.

"She'll ne'er get to see our baby. Oh, Sam, I shall miss her almost as much as if she were my mama."

Duffy was escorting Sam's mother down the hill, as Ruben was off hunting somewhere again. Their thoughts also seemed to be on the baby which was expected in the fall.

"There's never been a woman that loved babies any more than my Aunt 'Cille did," Duffy choked, finally realizing that his tears didn't make him any less of a man. "It's a downright shame that she never got word 'bout Little Marc's baby. And now she'll not see Libby's either."

Mrs. Kelly spoke in a shaky voice. "I only hope that I can live to ... oh, dear, ... Duffy, help me!" She stumbled against him, and when he reached for her hand, Duffy realized that the widow was now hot with fever. Automatically, he shouted.

"Mama! Come quick. She's sick!"

Everyone clustered around as Mrs. Kelly sort of folded up in Duffy's arms. Still alert, however, she sought out her son.

"Sam, keep Libby away! She mustn't take the illness."

Her constitution was much weaker than Lucille's had been. Before the week was through, the little group was again assembled at the top of the knoll, saying their final farewell to the Widow Kelly. Ruben had returned from his hunting spree empty-handed just hours after his mother's death. Immediately after the service, he told Sam goodbye and disappeared again.

"Somehow I feel as if I'll never see him again. The only reason he ever came home was to check in on Mama. My brother is a born frontiersman. I hope he finds happiness some day," Sam confided to his wife that night while they waited for sleep to enfold them.

"There's been so many changes so fast," replied Libby with her head resting on his chest. "Too many goodbyes. Y'know Sam, that's gonna be the best part of heaven for me. Never having to say goodbye." A tear plopped on his chest.

"It's hard to believe we'll be saying goodbye to Phillip tomorrow. How long have you all known him, Lib? It seemed his announcement today was such a shock to your mother."

"To Mama, yes. But Duffy told me he and Papa have known for a long time that Phillip didn't like farming. We've known him ... well, all of our lives, I guess. He'd sort of drift in and out. He and Aunt 'Cille had only been married a couple of years, though."

"He said he wants to see all the children and tell them in person about their mother. Will he go back to sea, do you think?"

"Well, you know what they say. Once a sailor, always a sailor. He says he's just going to get a small boat and do hauling on the River James. But I don't know."

They rearranged themselves to get more comfortable and were almost asleep when she spoke again. "Ooh— did you feel that?"

"He or she sure is a kicker, huh Lib? I ... sure do wish Mama could have lived ..." Now she felt the tears on her shoulder.

The summer was a good one for crops. Just the right amount of rain fell. The land was fertile and Will and Duffy were pleased with the yield from their acreage. The only cloud on the horizon seemed to be news from travellers, both those going up and down the rivers.

"Sounds as if we'll be at war with the motherland some day soon," Duffy said one evening after he'd talked with a trader on the bank that day. "Seems there are more and more little scuffles with the Redcoats happening back in the colonies."

His father interrupted him. "When I was fishing on the Elk River yesterday, the man I spoke with was more fearsome of an Indian war than a war for independence."

"Was it Chief Logan again?" Hannah asked looking up from the shawl she was repairing.

"Him and a bunch of other Shawnees," Will replied.

In the Kellys' cabin a similar conversation was taking place.

"I know we've ne'er had any trouble with them yet, Lib, but there's always a first time. You've got to see that yer father's suggestion is the only sensible thing to do. The Woodcutter's house is sittin' there empty. I'd feel so much better whilst I'm in the fields of a day if I knew yer ma was within shoutin' distance of ya."

"But Sam, this is our first home. I don't want to give up our privacy. And I wanted the baby to be born here in the first place you and I lived as man and wife."

He would not be persuaded. "The baby is another reason for us to move. We'd have ever so much more room."

"Oh, all right. I can see you've got your mind made up. And I remember back in Norfolk our vicar used to talk a lot about women being submissive to their husbands. So, I'll go," she grinned. "But I won't go willingly."

"Lib, if there is any truth in all the rumors from the north about that crazy Chief Logan, I'll feel lots better if we move over to the clearing."

Libby went on with her candlewicking, thinking the conversation had ended. But Sam interrupted her thoughts.

"And Libby, I want you to promise me that if you see any Indians you will go inside and bar the door and windows."

"Sam, don't be silly. I'm not afraid of the Indians. Why, don't you remember, just last week you traded some of our eggs to that one for a haunch of his deer meat?"

"Liberty Lucille Kelly . . ."

When she heard his tone, she knew she was licked. "All right!" she nearly shouted. "But I don't see what all the hubbub is about."

On October first along toward sunset, the hubbub Libby spoke about turned into a cacophony. Forty horsemen rode into their clearing at a full gallop.

"Yo—in the houses—are there any men about the place?"

Will and Sam opened their doors at precisely the same moment. Lib followed Sam out onto the porch, as did her Mama, Duffy, and Willy across the clearing.

"What's the meaning of this?" Will asked the man in the purple uniform who seemed to be in charge.

"Excuse me, sir. We didn't mean to descend on you like a horde. But of a truth, we came upon your homes almost afore we saw them."

"Why were you asking if there are men about?" Duffy asked.

Glancing from him back to his father, the colonel said, "Beggin' your pardon. I should have asked if there were any *young* men about!"

Libby caught her breath. Will looked as if he'd been slapped across the face. For the very first time in her life, Libby saw her father through the eyes of someone else. And now she realized that he did indeed look like an old man. His prematurely white hair, the stoop of his back, and his limp had been a part of her life forever.

"And what do you want with young men?" Sam asked, stepping off their porch.

"Well, sir, I am Colonel Andrew Lewis. These men are the militia from Augusta, Botetourt, and Fincastle counties. Under the orders of Lord Dunmore, we are marching up the Kanahwa River where we hope to engage Chief Cornstalk and the Shawnee, thereby making' this country a much safer place to raise your families." With this last, he cast sidelong glances at Libby's protruding belly.

"Who is Chief Cornstalk? All's we've e'er heard about is Chief Logan."

"Logan is makin' war, way up across the Ohio. But Cornstalk is swingin' farther south with his raids, into West Virginny here."

Until now only the colonel had spoken. But now another horseman broke away from the group on the edge of the clearing.

"Howdy, folks. I remember ya well. I sees the directions old Scotty gave ya got ya to where ya wanted ta go." Removing his hat and thereby revealing the flaming red hair, he jumped down to shake hands with Will.

"So, are you going on this Indian chase?" Will asked.

"Man, we've got ta. If we e'er want this country to be free from fear, we can't let 'em keep raidin'. Why, a rider heading south met up with us just last night and told of 'em takin' scalps at a place what can't be far from here, known as Burning Springs."

An audible gasp escaped all the settlers. Burning Springs was the nearest trading post to them.

Since the sun was nearly set, Will invited the soldiers to camp at their place, bedding down in the barn. The two families took supper together at no one's suggestion. They seemed to cling to each other out of desperation. At the end of the meal, Duffy arose.

"Papa, I'm goin' with them," he said, reaching for his gun to clean and oil it.

"I knew you would, son. Iffen I were younger . . . and more able-bodied . . ." he said sadly.

"Will, what are saying?" Hannah was indignant. "We can't let Duffy go! He's just a boy!"

Duffy never raised his voice. "Mama, I'm a man. And I can't let my family live in fear. We came here for freedom, and that's not true freedom—living afraid."

"I'm going, too," Sam said. "Now, Lib, don't go havin' a fit. It's not all that far to where they're marchin'. I've been there before. We'll just go up there and take care of this Cornstalk character and be back long afore yer time comes. Yer papa can protect you and yer ma."

159

Now little Willy spoke. "I'll go, too. I can fight In-juns." Holding up a make-believe musket he said. "Pow!"

Libby broke into tears. Hannah took her youngest on her lap.

" 'Fraid not, young man. Duffy and Sam I can't control ... but you will stay here with yer Papa and me."

Sam spoke again. "And can Lib have her old room back just for the few days we're gone?"

And so a resigned Libby and an unsteady Sam walked home at first dark to get ready for the early morning departure of the soldiers. Unable to sleep in the middle of the night, Libby stepped out onto the porch for some air.

"Hmmm, that's strange. They left the light burn in Mama's sewing room. I wonder why."

Her question was answered in the morning. She clung to Sam as long as she could. When he mounted up, she suddenly realized her brother was leaving too. Reaching up to hug him goodbye, she exclaimed, "Why, Duffy! What a beautiful muffler. The stripes are ... where did you get it?"

"Mama. I guess she worked on it all night. The white stripes—she unravelled the mitten sweater. Said I should wear it as the family's symbol of freedom." His voice cracked and his eyes were bright. "Go to her, Miss Liberty. She needs you."

It was so quiet in the clearing for the next two weeks that Libby thought she would lose her mind. Even Willy seemed subdued. She worked with Hannah on the baby's layette, but there was no joy in the task. Every ear seemed strained for the sound of either war or the soldiers returning.

On the sixteenth day a barge of men floated past. Will called out to ask of news.

" 'Twas a blood bath, sir!" a young voice responded.

160

"I guess we beat the Injuns, but we sure took lots of hits ourselves."

Early on the morning of the seventeenth, Lib looked out the upstairs window. A lone man was walking on the riverbank. His left arm was held against his body in a sling. Could it be?

"Sam, Sam ... are you hurt? Where's your horse? Where's Duffy?" she screamed as she ran awkwardly toward him.

Her husband lifted bloodshot eyes to hers. "Oh, Libby, I'm home," was all he could say.

That evening as they tended the tear in Sam's bicep where an arrow had miraculously passed through without hitting the bone, they heard the story of the battle of Point Pleasant in bits and pieces.

" 'Twas a week ago this morning," he began. It was the great Chief Cornstalk's own arrow which had hit Duffy. He knew this because the man's hair was so elaborately decorated with corn. "We were side by side, ma'am. I've asked myself a thousand times why it had to be him 'stead of me." He turned tortured eyes toward Hannah. After telling all about the battle and the signing of the treaty at the end which "opens up the Ohio country, north of the river for settlement" he returned to the story of Duffy.

"He didn't suffer none. 'Twas real quick," he went on with downcast eyes. "I pulled the arrow out, but 'tweren't no use. He reached up and pulled that little muffler off his throat and said, 'Tell Mama ... tell her it was ... for freedom!' And then he was gone."

All was silent except for gentle sobbing all around the room. At long last, Sam and Libby rose to go home.

Looking only at Will, Sam spoke in a low voice. "I buried him, Sir. They put most of 'em in a big common grave. I wanted to bring him home, but with losin' my horse and all, I couldn't. Do you remember that big Scot? He helped me dig a grave. And we put a big

161

rock over it. And I wrote Duffy Stivers and the date on it. I . . . I'm so sorry, Sir. Here's the . . ."

Will hugged him awkwardly as he took the muffler. "Thank you, Sam. We're grateful."

EPILOGUE

Another year had passed. Sam and Libby's little girl was walking already. They'd named her Diligency Destiny Kelly, but she was "Dilly" to everyone.

When Mama and Papa had confronted them with their news, Libby had hoped that the announcement of her second pregnancy would change their minds. But they would not be dissuaded.

"No, Liberty. It's just something we feel we must do. We shan't be far away. Just across the Ohio. Sam says you can get there in less than a week. We'll visit back and forth. But . . . your brother died to make the Ohio country free and your Papa always has wanted to live *in* Ohio. Since Lord Dunmore's war, more and more of the travellers are referring to this as West Virginny. I'll miss you, too, dear—but we'll get along."

And so, once again, there were goodbyes. It wasn't quite so hard since it wasn't the forever kind. But still there were tears as the small boat pulled away from shore heading north. Willy yelled, "Goodbye, Dilly" one more time as they went around the bend.

When they came to Point Pleasant, they searched for the landmarks Sam had told them about. When they found the rock, they stood arm in arm as their tears fell silently. Neither one could speak. Even the five-year-old knew instinctively to be quiet.

"My lady, I fashioned a marker. It's back on the boat. I'll go and get it."

"Let me stay here with him, Will. It's so peaceful."

"I'll take Willy," he replied.

It took him nearly an hour to return. The cross was

heavy, and even though he had put it on a handcart to tote it, he needed frequent rests. But Hannah was glad for the time to say goodbye to her firstborn.

He dug quite deep into the earth just north of the stone. When it was all in place, he sighed. "What do you think, my lady?" As per his instructions, she had not looked until now.

There was a large square below the crosspiece. In beautiful chiseling it read, "Freedom Duffy Stivers— 1757-1774—He died for his first name."

Hannah stared transfixed, and finally choked, "It's perfect, Will. But I brought something too. I know the weather will ruin it. But somehow, it seems fitting to leave it here—with him." So saying, she pulled from her reticule the little striped muffler made from the yarn of freedom. She tied it lovingly around the cross. Will noticed there were still some blood stains on the white yarn.

As they walked back toward the boat, Willy ran up a little hill.

"Pa! Look!" he shouted. "It's a mighty big river over there!"

Hannah and Will smiled through their tears.

"Yes, son. It's the Ohio," Will replied.